Through the Eyes of
Coventry Child
1939–1945

Through the Eyes of a Coventry Child
1939–1945

Ann Harris

First published in Great Britain in 2005
by Palm of Your Hand Press
www.palmofyourhandpress.co.uk

Copyright 2005 Ann Harris
The right of Ann Harris to be identified
as the author of this work has been asserted by her in
accordance with the Copyright, Designs and Patents Act 1988.

In some cases it has not been possible to trace ownership of illustrative
and written material used in this book. The publisher apologises
for any inadvertent omissions.

10 9 8 7 6 5 4 3 2

ISBN 0-9551150-0-0
ISBN 978-0-9551150-0-4

A CIP catalogue record for this book
is available from the British Library.

Printed in Great Britain by Warwick Printing Company
Caswell Road, Leamington Spa, Warwickshire.

This paperback is sold subject to the condition that it
shall not, by way of trade or otherwise, be lent, resold,
hired out, or otherwise circulated without the publisher's
consent in any form of binding or cover other than
that in which it is published and without a similar
condition including this condition being imposed
on the subsequent purchaser.

'The gaunt ruins of St Michael's Cathedral, Coventry, stare from the photographs, the voiceless symbol of the insane, the unfathomable barbarity which has been released on Western civilisation.'
The New York Tribune
November 1940

For those who still remember.

Chapter 1

'This country is at war.'

Neville Chamberlain

The Sunday war was declared turned out to be a warm and sunny day. It shouldn't have been. To be in sympathy with the rest of Europe it should have been damp and gloomy with storm clouds gathering overhead. But it wasn't. September 3rd 1939 was a beautiful autumn day.

All along the street, windows were opened early and the sound of a wireless came from nearly every home. On the Sabbath day this was unusual but no one complained. The German army had invaded Poland two days previously and everyone knew it would only be a matter of time before the news they all dreaded was broadcast.

Meg's father had switched on his wireless at dawn. He kept the volume down low, but she could still hear it as she lay in bed waiting for someone to come and tell her to get up. No one came: even her brother seemed to have forgotten her.

Turning on to her stomach, Meg carefully slid off the side of the bed and, still in her nightdress, padded softly downstairs. This was usually frowned upon and Meg's mother would get quite cross when she was disobeyed. Her father, a gentle man, would sometimes say quietly, 'She's only a little girl,' and then her mother would get cross with him too. It happened quite often these days. There were, though, some happier times when her mother would say something funny and make them all laugh. Then she would relax and look pretty. After that sunny Sunday her mother began to laugh even less, and gradually over the following years it didn't seem to matter much any more.

That morning, when Meg entered the kitchen, the table had already been laid for breakfast as usual but, when she was lifted on to her chair without a word of reprimand, Meg knew something was wrong. Her brother, John, didn't even glance at her.

Something really was wrong.

By the time Meg finished eating the bread and jam her mother gave her and drank the cup of warm milk that she hadn't wanted, some of the neighbours were already drifting in through the back garden gate. This was always left open on Sunday mornings so that her father's friends could wander in to have a chat with him if they felt like it.

Many of the men who lived in that area worked in the car industry, either at the nearby Humber Factory or the Morris Motor Company. Usually those who owned cars of their own would have been out in the back entry, cleaning their vehicles on such a lovely morning, but today no one seemed to have the heart for it. By eleven o'clock the men were joined by some of the women, who in normal circumstances would have been in their own kitchens cooking the Sunday dinner. None of them wanted to be on their own when the news came through.

When Neville Chamberlain said, 'This country is at war with Germany,' everyone went quiet. Meg saw her father put his elbows on the table and rest his head in his hands. When he glanced up and noticed the worried look on her face, he said, 'Don't worry, lass,' and ruffled her hair. He seemed to be addressing Meg, but at the same time he was looking at his wife. She thought her mother may have been crying but knew that this wasn't possible. Her mother never cried.

Many years later Meg was to remember how her mother had reacted when she'd heard the news that war had begun. At the time her grandfather was talking about Meg's mother's earlier life. He said that when she was seventeen she had started walking out with a young soldier. They hadn't been able to spend much time together before he was sent to the trenches and was killed just before the end of the First World War.

'He was her first beau,' Meg's grandfather said.

Then he added, 'Those who have been touched by war always stand in its shadow.'

The old man didn't need to continue.

By then Meg already knew this to be true.

Neville Chamberlain became Prime Minister in 1937, but his policy of appeasement failed to prevent the outbreak of World War II.

He believed that in war there are no winners, only people who do not lose.

In May 1940, after the Germans had invaded Holland and Belgium, he resigned the Premiership and Winston Churchill took his place.

Chamberlain died a few months later at a time when Britain itself was under threat. He was buried at Westminster Abbey on the 14th November 1940 – the day of the Coventry Blitz.

Chapter 2

'Coventry that do'st adorne the country wherein I was borne.'

Michael Drayton (1563–1631)

THE THREE SPIRES, COVENTRY.

The Coventry of old was a city of many contrasts and still retained much of its medieval past.

    Meg's grandfather, who had been brought up on a small farm in Spon End by his grandparents, knew the old city very well. The crumbling buildings, which had stood for hundreds of years along the ancient routes of Smithfield Street, High Street, Earl Street, Broadgate and Cross Cheaping, were part of his boyhood. He often said that he had been sent to the market in Cross Cheaping so many times as a boy that he thought he could walk there with his eyes shut. On the way he would sometimes stop to play by the River Sherbourne. Parts of the river that ran through the city were still accessible when he'd been a boy, but he said that it was always full of rubbish and the water smelled so foul that he never stayed there for more than a few minutes. Meg's grandfather also remembered finding parts of the old wall which had once surrounded Coventry. He said that it originally had twelve gates, but only two remained standing: one in Cook Street and the other, the Swanswell Gate, in Lady Herbert's Garden.

Meg sometimes saw this gate herself when she was taken into the garden after going to see the fire engines which often stood outside the fire station in Hale Street. She liked watching the firemen cleaning their vehicles. They would polish the engines until Meg could see her face in the red paintwork. Sometimes, if she was lucky, one of the men would lift her up on to one of the engines close to where the big brass bell was hanging.

During the war, whenever she heard the insistent clanging of a fire engine bell, she thought of her friends, the firemen, hanging on to their machines as they tried to get through the streets on their way to a fire.

Her grandfather, of course, remembered the days when the old steam fire engine was pulled by horses. Meg would have loved to have seen that.

She didn't remember the old Coventry at all, as much of it had already disappeared before the war started. However, there were still a few small areas, tucked away behind newer buildings that time seemed to have forgotten. Crowded courtyards, where the ribbon weavers had once lived and worked, still existed in Little Park Street and Much Park Street, although the conditions in which the inhabitants existed were very poor. But then they always had been.

In Victorian times, there were men who had tried to improve the lives of the people who came to Coventry in order to work. Meg's great-great-grandfather had known Joseph Cash, a Quaker, who with the encouragement of the editor of the local paper helped to make working conditions better for these poorly paid workers. Joseph Cash established in Hillfields a triangle of weavers' houses with workshops on the top floors. He'd even placed a steam engine in the backyard to provide power for their homes.

Rotherhams, who had a watch-making business in Spon Street, close to where Meg's family then lived, also established a cottage industry. Meg came to know their shop quite well. Later, as the war continued, bombing raids kept affecting the mantelpiece clock – her mother's pride and joy. Many-a-time, Meg had been taken in the pushchair to Rotherham's repair shop in Spon Street with her hands clutched tightly around the defective clock.

When Meg's paternal grandmother had been a girl in Royal Leamington Spa, she had borrowed her brother's bicycle and ridden it down the Parade. Before she got to the bottom of the hill, she was stopped by a gentleman who made her dismount, saying it was unseemly for a female to be seen riding a bicycle in public.

The bike she was riding had been made in Coventry by the Coventry Machinists' Company. This company had been started by James Starley, who also produced the penny-farthing bicycle.

Meg's family, like nearly every other family in Coventry, had benefitted by this upsurge in the city's fortunes. At one time there were more than a hundred cycle manufacturers in the city but, in 1896, the production of motorcars began.

Many of the old buildings in the centre of town were soon turned into car factories. Humber and Co began manufacturing in Lower Ford Street and the main Daimler factory was at Radford. The Deasy Motor Car Company was taken over by John Siddeley and later became part of Armstrong-Siddeley. By the turn of the century both Rover and the Riley Cycle Company were producing tricars and soon the Standard Motor Company and Lea-Francis also started producing three-cylinder cars.

There were many skilled engineers, whose talents became invaluable during both world wars. When Meg was much older and began to see a new and different city arising from the ruins, she realised that without such men Coventry might never have survived the war. Although its citizens endured terrible hardship, they had previously lived through times of inspiration and great energy on which they were able to draw when needed.

The men Meg knew as a child were proud to be engineers and manufacturers. The skills her grandfather possessed as a toolmaker stood him in good stead all his life and, when he died, a box of his handmade tools still remained by the side of his chair. There hadn't been many everyday problems Grandpa hadn't been able to solve with the aid of his toolbox.

There had been a market place in Coventry at Cross Cheaping since the thirteenth century. 'Cheaping' is an old English term for market. It originated from the word 'ceap' which meant to barter or bargain.

The wall, which had been built around Coventry in the fourteenth century, was destroyed in the seventeenth century after the city had harboured rebels during the Civil War.

By the beginning of the 1800s nearly a quarter of Coventry's population were weavers, many of whom lived in the new village of Hillfields.

The man who helped Joseph Cash improve the lives of the weavers was Charles Bray, Editor of **The Coventry Herald***, who was himself the son of a ribbon manufacturer. He and his wife were lifelong friends of the writer, George Eliot, who often visited them at their house, 'Rosehill', on the Radford Road.*

Chapter 3

'Dusk is the edge of darkness.'

The winter of 1940 was extremely cold with deep snow for most of January.

As the war spread all over Europe, people were urged to prepare themselves for the worst and Meg's father decided it was time the family had its own air-raid shelter. He wasn't able to install one until the weather was warm enough for the ground to soften, but he got everything ready in the garden.

Sir John Anderson, the Home Secretary, had approved a 'simple' design that was supposed to be easy to erect but turned out to be quite a problem, and a neighbour offered to help. Before they could even start constructing the shelter, a very deep hole had to be dug so that a large part of it would be below ground level. Everyone had to assist in this, including Meg whose job it was to carry buckets of soil away to spread around the flower borders.

John grumbled that the war would be over before they'd got the thing finished. He could well have been right except for the timely arrival of one of Meg's uncles, who seemed to have a better understanding of the instructions. With his assistance, they managed to bolt the six curved-steel sheets together at the top to form a tunnel-like structure and to figure out that one end had to be covered by the remaining flat piece of metal. This was supposed to be unbolted in an emergency to provide an exit if necessary. Even Meg's father had to agree that if he ever had to take it off the whole shelter would probably collapse. He said it was only standing upright because it was in a deep hole.

'Let's hope we don't ever have an emergency,' he said. As it happened there were to be many emergencies, but the end piece was never removed.

The Anderson shelter, or Andy as the children called it, may have been bombproof, but it certainly didn't look inviting. Meg's father made some seats out of upturned box crates and wooden planks, but it looked, and always was, cold and uncomfortable. Her mother left some candles and matches in an old biscuit tin just inside the entrance. She told Meg that many people never had the benefit of electric lights and had to use candles every night, so it shouldn't be a hardship for her family to have to use them occasionally.

Meg wasn't impressed. She'd already had a scary experience with candlelight. Sometimes, when she couldn't get to sleep, John would sit on her bed and tell her stories. She would pull the eiderdown over her head, leaving a little gap so that she could still hear what he said. Once, when he was telling her a rather gruesome story, they heard the noise of a cat howling in the garden next door. John immediately said it belonged to a witch. That night Meg had a terrible nightmare. She woke up suddenly and saw the shadows cast on the wall by the flame of the night light which stood on her bedside table. Meg was so frightened that for a short while she was unable to move. In the morning, when her mother came to get her up, Meg handed her the box of unused night lights and said that, as she was no longer a baby, she wouldn't be needing them any more.

Meg certainly didn't intend to watch any shadows made by flickering candlelight in this horrible shelter. She didn't think she would bother going down there in the dark very often.

As it turned out, Meg was to spend many happy daylight hours playing in and around the Anderson shelter. Her father covered the top of the structure with some of the excavated soil and in the spring he planted vegetables – carrots, potatoes, cabbages and onions. He also put up a row of sticks so that in the late summer they would be able to have some runner beans. This was done partly to improve the view from the house but mainly because, like everyone else in the neighbourhood, Meg's father was now 'Digging for Victory' as requested by the government. And Meg was helping him – well he let her think she was. She even had a small patch of her own to look after.

Having their own vegetables in the garden turned out to be very useful for the family. Although rationing of certain foods had been introduced at the beginning of the year, it was only later on that Meg's mother began to complain about shortages. She thought a meat allowance of one shilling and ten pence per person each week was hardly adequate, but the ration of half a pound of butter and half a pound of bacon per head was plenty, and she was able to make some tasty stews with their vegetables. It was in July when tea was rationed to two ounces per person per week that women began to realise how difficult things might become. Popping round to a neighbour's house for a cup of tea in the afternoon was one of life's little pleasures. Now it looked as if that was about to be taken away from them.

However, no one seemed to mind very much when the street lights no longer came on. Meg, being in bed early every night, didn't even know about it. Most people purchased a small torch and, if they needed to venture out after dark, they would dutifully point the beam of light down at the ground. Everyone heeded the warning that it was important not to assist any potential enemy action, so no chinks of light were allowed to be seen through the curtains at night. To make life easier, most people tried to get home before daylight faded.

Meg's father said he could still see some light coming from behind their curtains, and they had to purchase some blackout material to make blinds for every window in the house. It was impossible to make them look nice, so Meg's mother still hung her usual curtains up inside. Like most of her neighbours, she changed these winter and summer. It was a tradition. The lounge curtains were dark green velvet in the winter and light green brocade in the summer. Without fail and whatever the weather, they were changed at the end of October and the beginning of April every year. This routine would be strictly adhered to throughout the war, even though the windows were sometimes shattered during the air raids. At least, when all the panes eventually had taped crosses stuck on them to help contain any broken glass, Meg's mother ceased fretting about the Germans ruining her lovely curtains.

As with many other things, it would take more than the threat of an invasion to alter the habits of a lifetime.

It was around this time that Meg's father volunteered to be a warden. Like many other men who were too old to be in the army, he wanted 'to do his bit for the country'. As soon as dusk came, he patrolled the streets to ensure that all outside light was extinguished. 'Put that light out!' became the first of many wartime phrases, which Meg never forgot.

She thought at first her father was called an ARP because that was the name on the armband he always wore when on duty. But he told her that he was a warden and that ARP stood for air-raid precaution. Neither of them knew that, within a few months, the word 'precaution' would count for nothing as night after night he and others like him would be searching frantically for survivors in bomb-damaged buildings.

Street lights were switched off at the start of the war and not switched on again until after the war ended.

ARP wardens put their lives at risk every night they were on duty. Sometimes they would have to try and persuade confused and elderly people to leave their homes for a safer shelter. This became more difficult after the city started to suffer continual night-time raids. Everyone was tired and, as the war went on, some older people began to care less about their own safety. Couples sometimes just wanted to be left in their own homes 'to die together if it was meant to be'. Sadly, it also meant that occasionally a warden died with them while trying to convince them to leave.

In October 1940 an ARP warden in Coventry shepherded over two hundred people to safety in shelters before being killed himself.

Chapter 4

'He was my friend, faithful and just to me.'

William Shakespeare

One day, when Meg and her father were working on the vegetable patch, a boy wandered through the open back gate. He was older than John and looked thin and dirty, but his eyes were alert, looking from side to side and taking everything in. Meg's father looked at him warily but didn't say anything apart from a curt 'Hello'.

'What's your name?' the boy asked Meg, who was at the time sitting on the paving slabs by the dustbin removing worms from a pile of soil. Before she could answer, he asked her why she wasn't at school.

'I don't think I am old enough,' she replied. 'Why aren't you?'

'I don't need to go to school any more,' said the boy. 'I can read and write already. Can you read?'

'I can read a bit,' said Meg, 'but I can't do sums.'

'My dad says that, if I was meant to do sums, God would have given me a brain,' the boy said triumphantly. 'Have you got a brain?'

Meg thought carefully for a few moments. 'No, I don't think I have,' she said.

'Well then, that's probably why you can't do sums,' the boy replied amiably, sitting down beside her and helping with the worms.

This was the beginning of a special time for Meg. She had never really had a friend of her own before. Most of the neighbourhood children went to school and, although she would sometimes go over the road to visit a lady who had a new baby, there was no one of her own age to talk to.

The boy, who said his name was Thomas but that she could call him Tom, started to come fairly regularly through the back gate. Meg would often be in the garden waiting for the rattle of the catch being lifted. Sometimes the bolt hadn't been drawn back and he couldn't get in. She wasn't tall enough to reach it herself and would run into the kitchen to fetch her mother. Often the boy had gone before they got there.

Tom was an odd boy and Meg soon realised that her parents weren't too sure about letting her play with him. Her father went to great lengths to try and glean some information about his home life from him, but he said that it was like getting blood out of a stone. Tom wouldn't say where he lived exactly, but he did mention once that he was staying for the time being with his grandmother who lived near Gosford Green. Meg knew the park fairly well as they often walked through it on the way to visit her own grandparents in Stoke Heath. There was a bandstand in the middle of the park and she and her brother would sometimes climb on to it and pretend to play different musical instruments until the park keeper noticed them and made them get down.

In spite of her father's efforts, Tom wouldn't elaborate further, indicating that it was only for a short time while his mother got things sorted out. What things he didn't say.

After a few days, Meg's mother took pity on him and often, when he arrived unannounced in the mornings, she gave him a mug of tea and a slice of bread and jam. She said to her husband you could tell he was under-nourished and not very well looked after judging by the state of his clothes. But she had often seen boys looking worse than this when she had been growing up in the years before the Great War. And she had also seen them when, not much older than Tom, they had marched off to fight in 'the war to end all wars', some of them wearing the only new outfit they'd ever had in their lives.

Once, when Tom was sitting on the bench by the kitchen door wolfing down his breakfast, Meg's mother asked him if he had a father. He just nodded and then, rather surprisingly, put his mug down on the paving slabs and reached into his pocket, pulling out a small, dog-eared photograph of a thin-faced, rather grave-looking soldier. It was difficult to see a look of Tom about him except the poverty, which had obviously shaped both their lives.

'He's in the army then,' said Meg's mother, studying it carefully as he handed it to her.

'Yes, he is,' Tom said, taking back the photograph. Then, as he put it into his pocket, he added proudly, 'He's in the Royal Warwickshire Regiment. He volunteered. He didn't wait to be called up.'

She smiled as she slowly nodded her head, understanding his pride.

It was the first and last time Tom ever gave any information about himself, but it made a big difference as far as Meg was concerned. After that morning, Tom was treated like one of the family. The bolt on the back of the gate was always undone first thing so that he was able to get in if he chose to come, though they never knew for certain that he would. When he did arrive, he would have his breakfast at the kitchen table like the rest of them and, best of all, Meg sometimes saw his father slip him sixpence when he thought no one was looking. She knew deep down that her mother wouldn't have approved of this and she wasn't sure John would either, so she never mentioned it. It was one of the small secrets that gave her pleasure in later years, when she remembered the look on Tom's face as her father winked at him and gave him a sixpenny bit.

For a short time, life in the Midlands seemed almost normal as the impact of war being declared gradually lessened. The expected air raids hadn't happened and the news from Europe, although disturbing, was something other people knew more about. For a little girl, who now had a friend of her own, life was how it should be.

Meg was grateful for the fact that, although her mother kept chiding Tom about not going to school, he still kept appearing at the back gate. It didn't happen every day and he didn't explain where he went to on the days he didn't appear. 'I might go to school then or I might not,' was all he said when questioned.

Meg didn't mind where he went as long as he kept coming back. Neither of them bothered about the age gap. Tom seemed to know about such a lot of things and willingly shared his knowledge with her. He pointed out the different birds that landed on the birdbath in the garden. The robin was easy, but she also learned how to recognise a blackbird and a starling and the sound of a thrush which sometimes perched on the roof of her home. It wasn't so much the fact that he taught her these things that pleased Meg but that he bothered with her at all. He didn't tease her like John and his friends often did.

One of the few toys she possessed was an old wooden farmyard which had been handed down from her brother. Some of the animals were missing and bits of the fencing broken, but Tom would patiently set the whole farm up for her placing the remaining animals in their correct positions. Then he would make her laugh by mimicking the sounds they were supposed to make.

When it became almost impossible to find any toys left in the shops to buy, Meg's father, after a long search, managed to get a doll for her birthday. It was the only doll she ever possessed but, when she started playing with it, the eyes, which were made to blink, fell back inside the head. Tom, with his thin fingers, managed to manoeuvre the eyes back into place and glue them in position. It wasn't the same, of course, but at least Meg still had a doll to play with.

Tom was good at doing things like that, but Meg liked it best when he turned up with an old drawing pad. Most of the pages had been used before and someone had rubbed out the existing pictures so that Tom was able to create his own drawings.

One day, just after Easter, he borrowed a pencil stub from her mother and then sketched each of the family in a different way. He got Meg to sit still on the garden bench while he drew a picture of her with the flowering currant bush blossoming in the background. John was made to look like a reluctant schoolboy, which he was, and Meg's father like a benevolent old man, which was only partly right.

Then Tom suddenly said he had to go and abruptly closed his drawing pad. Without even saying goodbye, he went quickly out through the back gate.

'Well,' said Meg's father, glancing mischievously at her mother, 'he obviously couldn't face the thought of drawing you.'

This was a mistake. Meg's mother was not at all amused and she proceeded to spoil what had been a very pleasant day by not speaking to anyone for the rest of the evening.

But what happened the next morning made up for everything. Before the gate could be unbolted, the latch was rattled violently. It was a little while before John managed to get down to open it, but this time Tom hadn't gone away. He walked through the gate without saying a word. In one hand he had his drawing book and in the other he held a bunch of primroses.

'I picked these from the railway embankment,' he said to Meg's mother, 'and I've got this for you.' He pushed a piece of paper from his pad into her hands and was gone before anyone could say anything.

Meg's mother stood very still, gazing at the drawing Tom had given her. Then she silently turned it so that they could all see.

The boy had captured on the paper a mother that Meg didn't really know. Where was the reserved and unapproachable mother they saw everyday? Here was a woman with a softness in her eyes and a gentle smile touching her lips – a woman who must have existed at one time but for some reason had lost her way. It had taken a boy, who had only known her for a short while, to recognise that she was still there.

No one seemed to know what to say.

Meg's mother suddenly thrust the drawing at her father and turned to the cupboard to get an empty jam jar for the primroses. She took a long time at the kitchen sink to arrange the few flowers before placing them on the table and going upstairs.

It was not mentioned again and Meg never knew what happened to the drawing. She did notice, however, that the primroses were left in the jar on the kitchen table long after they were dead.

Easter Sunday was early in 1940 on the 24th March.

A few days later the German army invaded Denmark and Norway.

Wildflowers, being left undisturbed for years, grew in profusion over bombed areas and railway embankments.

> 'The flowers left thick at nightfall in the wood
> This Eastertide call into mind the men,
> Now far from home, who, with their sweethearts should
> Have gathered them and will never do again.'
>
> In Memoriam
> Philip Edward Thomas

Chapter 5

'And each slow dusk a drawing-down of blinds.'

Wilfred Owen

Tom's visits became less frequent after Easter. Meg's mother hoped it was because he was attending school more regularly, but she knew better than to ask him. He was a boy who never let his guard down, even for her. She could only guess at the events which must have driven him to put up such a barrier between himself and the outside world. At least when he was with her family he could behave like the boy he still was.

One day at the beginning of May he turned up just as they were about to leave on their weekly visit to see Meg's grandparents. It was too far for Meg to walk there and back so, much to her disgust, she had to go in the pushchair. As Meg's mother was carrying some shopping, Tom offered to help and he cheerfully pushed Meg all the way up Ball Hill. It wasn't far then to her grandfather's house and Tom agreed to come with them. Meg was pleased. She knew he'd like her grandparents. Grandma was a plump, gentle lady who smiled a lot and Grandpa, although he could get cross (he and Meg's mother didn't always get on), had some wonderful stories to tell about the old times. Their front door usually stood open during the day so that neighbours could drop in when passing. Grandma said it saved getting up and down all the time. Although Meg knew her mother didn't approve of this, she herself thought it was a

good idea, especially as she wasn't yet tall enough to open anyone's front door. Life at Grandpa's and Grandma's was less complicated than most other places she knew.

Then there were the sweets. When Meg went to visit, Grandpa would put his hand down the side of his big old chair and pull out a bag of sweets. Throughout the war, even when rationing made sweets scarce, there was always a few sweets for Meg and, as she got older, the occasional half-crown.

When Tom walked in with them that day, the sweets appeared immediately. Grandpa already seemed to know about Tom and was pleased to see him. He emptied the sweets into the little dish on the table and offered them to the boy first and Tom took a humbug – Grandpa's favourite. When Meg chose her sweet, a jelly baby, and promptly bit the head off it, Grandpa laughed. He said he used to do that a long, long time ago, when he was a young boy and Queen Victoria was still on the throne. It had been a special treat for a boy like him to be given a sweet and he made the most of it by always sucking each sweet very slowly. Grandpa told them that when the Victorians first made jelly babies they were called 'unclaimed babies'. This so upset some of the ladies that the production of these sweets was eventually stopped until Bassett's started making them again after the First World War and renamed them 'peace babies'.

Meg was pleased to see Tom laughing at this, as he seldom laughed, but she didn't really mind what they were called just as long as she could carry on biting their jelly heads off.

Grandma, sitting quietly in her chair and smiling with pleasure at the children, insisted that Tom should stop and have some dinner with all of them. In their living room Meg's grandparents had a black, old-fashioned range which had an oven on each side of the fire. This fire was nearly always lit, even in the summer, and a kettle rested on the hob ready to heat up on the glowing coals. Although there was a small gas cooker in the kitchen, Grandpa always insisted that the meat should be cooked

in one of the fireside ovens. He chose the meat at the butcher's himself and always supervised the cooking. When it was cooked to perfection, he sharpened his carving knife and made everyone sit round the table while he carefully lifted the thin slices on to the plates. As he poured the thick gravy over the meat, he always said the same thing: 'A feast, rich for a king.' No one ever took any notice of him – they were already too busy tucking in.

Grandpa had an allotment at the back of Gosford Green near the railway lines and, before he became crippled with arthritis, he managed to grow his own vegetables there. Meg always thought that no one made more tasty meals than her grandparents and that day Tom must have thought the same. He ate so much dinner that he had to have a rest before they could return home. Grandpa didn't mind as he obviously liked the boy. He started telling Tom about his own childhood.

He said that, while he had been living with his grandparents on their small farm in Spon End, one of his tasks had been to fetch any cattle that had strayed from the field and been put into the pound on Top Green. He and Tom both laughed at the problems this had caused him over the years. Trying to manoeuvre a cow down the Warwick Road and through the town, even without any traffic, was no mean task for a young lad.

He also told Tom about the time he had spent as a cadet at Coventry Barracks, serving under Superior Barrack Sergeant Kitson. He said that Sergeant Kitson was a very strict man but fair. Grandpa had obviously admired him very much, especially after the Sergeant had taught him to ride a horse. Perhaps it was this, plus the fact that Grandpa had been brought up on a farm, that made him buy a horse not long after he was married. Grandma had told him in no uncertain terms that they couldn't afford to keep a horse, so he'd sold it and bought a motorcycle instead. He didn't say what Grandma had thought about that and, when Tom glanced at her, she just smiled and gently shook her head. Grandpa went on to say that he had been one of the first men in Coventry to own a motorcycle. He was very proud of that.

Meg found out, when she was older, that her grandfather had every right to feel proud of what he had achieved. He had never spoken about it himself, but he had been born out of wedlock and his father, who did eventually marry his mother, died at the age of thirty-two. That was why Meg's grandfather had been raised by his grandparents and, although he had been a bright scholar, there was not enough money to allow him to stay at school. Meg never knew what had become of his mother. But it later helped her to understand why her grandfather had been so nice to Tom on that happy afternoon. He had recognised a kindred spirit.

When Meg's mother indicated that they really must go, Grandpa stood up, put his hand on Tom's shoulder and said to him quietly, 'I think you're having a bad time at the moment, lad. If that's the way of it, always remember you're a Coventry kid, like me. We Coventry kids are good at surviving.'

With that, he gave Tom a pound note. Tom didn't say anything. He couldn't. He just looked at Grandpa and nodded before turning away. Meg gazed at them in amazement. She had never had a whole pound to herself but it didn't matter. She just knew that it had been a good day.

Meg never spent any more happy days with Tom. The situation in Europe was now very grave and the wireless in the kitchen was kept switched on from morning till night. Sometimes Meg's mother would suddenly sit down without taking off her apron and just listen to it. The look on her face often worried Meg.

The weather was warm and sunny, but they seldom went out and, when they did, it was only to the local shop and the Co-op.

One morning Meg's father went into work late so that he could listen to the eight o'clock news. He called upstairs to her mother to say that Mr Chamberlain had resigned and Winston Churchill had become Prime Minister.

As the weeks passed without Tom appearing at the back gate, Meg began to stop looking out for him so often. She spent much of her time in the garden, sowing some flower seeds in her own little patch and looking after the vegetables.

Then one bright morning Meg awoke to find sunlight streaming into the room. John had already gone to school so she knew it must be getting late, and she wondered why no one had come to tell her to get up.

She could hear her father talking softly to her mother. He should have left for work by now. Feeling worried, as she so often did these days, Meg slipped out of bed and, wearing just her nightdress, went into the front room. Her parents stopped talking as soon as they saw her. Meg became vaguely aware that the blinds were still down, which filled her with dread. Young though she was, she knew that, when someone in the family or neighbourhood died, the windows at the front of the house would remain covered as a sign of respect. She hated the thought of anyone dying. She couldn't understand where they went.

Her father, seeing the look on her face even in the gloom, knelt in front of her and held her hands. 'It's all right. There's nothing for you to worry about,' he said. 'It's just very sad news for Tom. His father has been killed fighting the enemy in France so won't be coming home. We've all got to think about Tom now and be especially kind to him when he comes.'

Meg didn't know how she could be especially kind and thought instead that she would save some of her sweets as a present for him. But Tom never came.

'His mother needs him at home,' her father said, not realising how much this hurt Meg. Didn't he understand that she needed him too?

Meg's friendship with Tom became the first of many she made during the war years that didn't last long. Eventually she learned to deal with this by not having one particular friend but always being part of a crowd, which usually worked out quite well.

But there was a happy ending to this particular friendship. A few years after the war, an envelope dropped through the letterbox with an Australian stamp on it. There was only a single sheet of notepaper inside which was addressed to them all. It was from Tom. It explained that he had emigrated to Australia on the assisted passage scheme and had been working on various farms in the outback, a hard life but one which suited him well. Tom didn't go into details, nor did he mention his own family, but he wrote that he had never forgotten the kindness Meg's family had shown towards him.

He ended the short letter by asking them to pass on a message to Grandpa. Tom just wanted him to know that, although he was now living in Australia, he was still a Coventry kid at heart.

Winston Churchill became Prime Minister of Great Britain on Friday, 10th May 1940.

On 26th May the Royal Warwickshires were part of the British Expeditionary Force who were ordered to fight a rearguard action enabling the embarkation of the allied troops at Dunkirk.

On Tuesday, 28th May, after fighting a heroic battle, many of them were captured by the German army, herded into a cowshed outside the town of Wormhout and massacred.

Of the hundred or so men who were part of that massacre, fifty were members of the Royal Warwickshire Regiment.

Chapter 6

'Never in the field of human conflict was so much owed by so many to so few.'

Winston Churchill

When in September 1939 everyone had been told to make preparations for war, Meg's parents decided that it would be best if both children were to sleep downstairs. This meant moving the two single iron bedsteads into the backroom overlooking the garden. It also meant that John and Meg would be sharing a room for the first time.

Meg liked this new arrangement, but John complained noisily. Their mother told him that in the circumstances it was a small price for him to pay and, this way, she would be able to make sure that they both got up quickly in the night, if necessary. She didn't explain anything further. What made it worse for John was the fact that for months the only planes that flew directly overhead were British ones, so he thought there was no need for him to be stuck downstairs with Meg.

Then, in the summer of 1940, the threat of an invasion became real. The Battle of Britain began in earnest and aerial warfare raged day after day in the skies above the South of England.

John couldn't contain his excitement. He kept annoying everyone by mimicking *Just William*, saying, 'Sleep? I jolly well wouldn't waste an air raid by sleeping through it!' His only worry was that the war would be over before he became old enough to be a pilot. At the age of ten, John still had a few years to go, but after 1940 any man who wore the blue uniform of the RAF was a hero to John, and pilots were special.

Early one morning, when they were both outside in the street, John grabbed Meg's arm and pointed at the sky. In the far distance she could just make out the figure of a man dangling from a parachute. Her brother frowned and said that the plane must have already come down over open countryside. They remained watching for ages.

'I hope he lands safely,' he added quietly. There was no way of knowing whether the airman was one of ours or one of theirs – at that moment it didn't seem important. The war was still a source of excitement for them.

John told Meg that some RAF bomber pilots left the top button of their tunics undone when flying in combat. This was so that, if a plane crashed with a crew on board, the pilot could be identified as the one flying the plane. He'd got this information from a young man who lived two doors down the street from them. Meg's mother called this young man 'a daredevil'. He was the only person the children knew who owned a motorbike and sometimes he would ride it up and down the entry that ran along the backs of the houses. If he noticed the children watching him, as they often did, he would suddenly get up and balance on the saddle while the motorbike was still going at full throttle. It would only be for a second or two, although to Meg it seemed much longer, but it meant that John was in total awe of him. Not long after the war started the young man joined the RAF and that was the end of the free entertainment in the alley.

One afternoon, when only Meg and her mother were at home, the young man knocked on their front door and told them that he had leave to come back to see his mother before reporting for duty again that night. He didn't say where he was going. No one in the forces was ever allowed to reveal that information. It was said, 'Careless talk costs lives.'

Unfortunately there was no one in at his house so he came in to wait. He looked very handsome in his uniform and Meg's mother fussed over him, even getting out the lace tablecloth and best china. Despite the rationing, a plate of thinly cut slices of bread and real butter quickly appeared on the table as if by magic, and a jar of strawberry jam and an opened tin of sardines were strategically placed by the pilot's elbow ready for him to make a choice. He hungrily helped himself to two slices of bread and butter, carefully scraped some strawberry jam on top and then, to Meg's amazement and absolute delight, emptied the whole tin of sardines over the lot. After two mugs of scalding hot tea, he thanked Meg and her mother profusely and went home.

They never saw him again.

One day a month or so later, Meg overheard her father talking to John about the young man. Suddenly her brother brushed past her and ran upstairs, banging the door behind him. John never spoke about what had happened but, years later, when he and Meg were walking together across the Memorial Park playing fields, they found under one of the cherry trees a plaque which bore the young pilot's name. Silently, John bent down and touched it.

'I never got the chance to say goodbye,' he said after a while. 'I always hoped that one day, when I grew older, he and I might have become real friends.'

The war deprived many such people of the capacity for friendship, because friendships demand a future and some only had moments to give.

The Battle of Britain officially started on 10th July 1940.

During the next few months, the loss of crew members and aircraft on both sides was devastating.

Many thousands of civilians were also killed or injured during the air raids at this time.

At the end of October the German air force, having taken by far the heaviest losses, was forced to abandon the attempt to gain control of Britain in this way.

The Battle of Britain was won at great cost and officially declared at an end on the 31ˢᵗ October 1940.

The camaraderie that existed among aircrews was exceptional and RAF pilots sometimes found a way of remembering their own comrades. Early in the war a parcel dropped from an RAF plane over occupied Holland contained a wreath with a message asking for it to be placed on the grave of P. Rohan who had been shot down over the island of Rosenberg. The Free Dutch newspaper was able to confirm that this request had been successfully carried out.

> *'Say, not in grief,*
> *that they are no more.*
> *But, in thankfulness,*
> *that they were.'*

Chapter 7

'Twilight and evening bell,
And after that the dark!'

Alfred, Lord Tennyson

'John,' said Meg timidly. She was trying to put the buttons of her liberty bodice into the right holes, but it was all too difficult for her this morning. 'Have you got to go to school again today?'

'Don't be stupid! Of course I've got to go to school,' her brother shouted crossly. 'I go to school on Mondays, Tuesdays, Wednesdays, Thursdays and Fridays. It's Monday today so I'M GOING TO SCHOOL.'

His voice was getting louder and louder as he spoke. A tear trickled slowly down Meg's nose. She was very tired, they all were, and she struggled to put her knickers on without toppling over.

In a few short weeks Meg had had to grow up. No one now had much time for her in the mornings, so she managed the best she could. She climbed on to her chair and washed her face and hands in the bowl of cold water, which her mother had placed on the kitchen table, and dried herself on a rather grubby towel.

This would have been frowned upon a few months previously, but it was becoming impossible for her mother to cope with housework like she used to. Air-raid warnings occurred frequently and, even if as sometimes happened, they were followed quite quickly by the All Clear, disturbed nights became common. It made everyone irritable in the mornings. Everyday life was becoming increasingly difficult for all the mothers in their neighbourhood. Food rationing meant that meals were not the happy occasions the children were used to and it also meant that it would be years before Meg got to taste many quite ordinary foods.

Her father was usually given the bacon ration. He needed a good breakfast before he went to work, especially if he had been on warden duty all night. Her mother used to swap the cheese ration with a neighbour for sugar as the family all had a sweet tooth. So Meg was able to have sugar in her tea but never tasted cheese. She quite liked the powdered egg that her mother used, and at least they had the fresh vegetables that her father grew in the garden. So, even with the small meat ration, they always had one good meal a day. However, it meant continually trying to eke the rations out without much room for variety. Gradually Meg's mother became more and more irritable and sometimes withdrawn. She began to complain about small things, especially when the chimes on public clocks were stopped. Even though they had a clock on the mantelpiece, she said she would no longer be able to tell the time by listening out for the Council House clock to strike. She even hated it when the church bells no longer rang out on Sundays, even though she seldom went to church herself. She said that she'd put up with only being allowed four inches of water to bathe in, there being no street lighting and everything else, but this was too much! It was as if, knowing that she could do nothing about the really upsetting events that were taking place almost daily, she concentrated on grumbling about the small things instead. But she did get some pleasure from listening to the wireless. This was always switched on in their house and Meg knew better than to interrupt the programme that started, 'Here is the news and this is Alvar Liddell reading it.' Mr Liddell spoke with a very calm voice, even when the news was bad. And sometimes it was very bad indeed.

It was very bad that day, when she had trouble getting dressed and John was cross about having to go to school. Meg was sitting at the kitchen table in the evening when the news programme came on the wireless. A man with a sombre voice said that a ship with many evacuee children on board had been torpedoed six hundred miles from land. When Meg's mother heard this she got up and ran out into the garden. When she came back in she didn't say anything. Later their father told a subdued John and Meg that this war was particularly hard on women. He said that their mother had been brought up at a time when women had watched their young husbands march off to the First World War and many of them were now having to watch their sons do the same. It was very sad that some of these women might also be losing their grandchildren. John said that it must have been terrible for all those evacuee children on that boat.

John now grumbled most mornings, saying that he was too tired to go to school. It didn't make any difference. He had to go all the same. One of the things that remained constant throughout the forthcoming turbulent years was that, if the school managed to open, their mother made sure that John and later Meg attended.

Sometimes this seemed ridiculous. Once, after a heavy raid, Meg was put into the old pushchair and bounced over broken bricks and other debris so that her mother could get John to school. When they eventually got there, they found the whole area cordoned off as an unexploded bomb had landed on the green in front of the building. Meg's mother was very cross with John because he said it was a pity it hadn't gone off. That day they went to see Grandma instead.

It wasn't the only time that Meg came into close proximity with an unexploded bomb. When air attacks on Coventry got worse in August 1940, communications suffered and, after each raid, people began to worry about what might have happened to their relatives and friends. Often the only way of finding out was by cycling or walking to the affected areas in the city. Meg's mother did this quite often, eventually becoming part of a community network which passed on information by word of mouth. Meg became quite used to being pushed first thing in the morning to see how various relatives were. The trouble was that her mother, who was tired after being up most of the night, would take the shortest route even if it meant ignoring the 'keep out' notices. Once a policeman saw her pushing Meg across an area that had been cordoned off. He shouted at her, 'You silly woman! Don't you realise that you've just pushed that child over an unexploded bomb? We don't come out in the middle of the night to put these ropes up because we enjoy it!'

Meg was petrified: not because she had been pushed over an unexploded bomb, but because an angry policeman had just called her mother 'a silly woman'.

That day they were going to check up on one of Meg's aunts. When they eventually managed to reach the house, it was in ruins. Bombs had destroyed the whole terrace as well as the junior school opposite. Everywhere was chaos, with some men trying to pull down walls that were deemed to be unsafe and others trying to shore up walls that could provide some protection. They were all too busy to answer Meg's mother's frantic questions, but someone told her that they were still searching in the rubble to see if anyone was trapped. After a while a lady, who had been wandering disconsolately around what was left of her home, told Meg's mother that they had all been in a communal shelter together and, to her knowledge, no one had been killed. But she didn't know where their relations were now.

Then, suddenly, Meg's mother looked down at her and smiled for the first time that day. 'We know where they'll be, don't we, Meg? They'll be at Grandpa's.'

As indeed they were.

Food rationing came into force on 8th June 1940 and didn't end completely until nine years after the war in 1954.

After June 1940 it was forbidden for church bells to be rung, so that they could be used, if necessary, to signal an invasion. However, on 15th November 1942 in a special programme, the bells from all the bombed cities were broadcast on the wireless.

On 17th September 1940 The City of Benares sank with ninety evacuee children and their carers on board. Eighty-one children died, five of them being from one family. On 25th September a lifeboat, carrying some of the surviving children, was sighted by a Sunderland flying boat. A small boy scout was able to signal 'City of Benares' with a handkerchief and a warship was diverted to pick them up.

Unexploded and delayed action bombs caused many deaths in Coventry. The bomb disposal squad was nicknamed the 'suicide squad' as so many of its volunteers were killed.

On 18th October 1940 a bomb being removed from Coventry to Whitley Common exploded as it was being placed in a prepared hole, killing five men. On 12th April 1941 a delayed action bomb exploded behind the Hippodrome, killing an officer and four of his men.

> 'Greater love hath no man than this.'

Chapter 8

'I am the enemy you killed my friend.'

Wilfred Owen

There was blood on the pavement. Meg peered through the wooden bars of the front gate and saw a huge pile of rubble where Mrs Watson's house had once stood. From somewhere high up, water was trickling out on to the shattered glass that littered the pavement. The dark velvet curtains, which had been Mrs Watson's pride and joy, dangled in strips from what was left of the window frame. This worried Meg a great deal because now everyone could see inside the old lady's home and she wouldn't like that.

Mrs Watson hadn't let the war affect her life in any way. She always stayed in her own bed at night, refusing to go into an air-raid shelter, saying that she had already survived one war and would be doing the same again, God willing. Anyway, she didn't agree with people killing one another. 'There's enough problems to sort out in the world without everyone fighting wars all the time,' she'd said one day when they were outside watering her garden. 'I wouldn't be surprised if there isn't someone just like me watering flowers in Germany at this very moment. That person won't be wanting anyone killed any more than I do.'

She looked down at Meg, as she always did when she needed to make a point. The little girl, who seldom understood what the old lady was talking about, had nodded her head vigorously in approval, basking in the importance of being consulted on what was obviously an important issue. She didn't receive that much attention at home.

Mrs Watson was very proud of the fact that she kept a tidy house. Every day of the week apart from Sunday she wore a pinafore with a duster in the pocket. She'd told Meg that this was so she could flick a speck of dust off the furniture whenever she saw one. Most of the other women in the street wore aprons, but Mrs Watson's mother had been a maid in a grand London house and had worn a white apron with a bib pinned on to the front of a black dress. She'd said it was called a *pin afore*. What had been all right for the Victorian gentry was good enough for Mrs Watson. *She* always wore a pinafore.

Meg began to wonder why the old lady wasn't already about with her duster. There was such a lot to do. Perhaps later she and her mother would go over and help tidy up just as they had done when Mrs Watson had been ill. Meg had enjoyed that. She had been allowed to dust some of the treasures that stood on the windowsill in Mrs Watson's front room. 'Clutter,' her mother had called these treasures when talking to her father later. Meg didn't know what clutter was, but she realised that it meant her mother didn't like them very much. Perhaps that was why they didn't have treasures at home. Meg loved all of them, from a pottery figure Mrs Watson called 'Prince Albert' to a little dish with the word 'Margate' printed on it. Mrs Watson said that she had bought this herself at a fair when she had gone to the seaside with her young man. This young man had later become Mr Watson. Meg said that one day she might go to a fair with a young man to buy herself a dish and get married. The old lady had laughed, saying it didn't happen like that and, anyway, there was always plenty of time.

Although Meg loved all of Mrs Watson's treasures, the thing she most enjoyed dusting was a small wooden carving of the Three Wise Monkeys. One monkey had his hands over his eyes, the middle one had his hands over his ears and the last one had his hands over his mouth. What had Mrs Watson said about them? 'See no evil. Hear no evil. Speak no evil.'

'One day, when I'm gone, this treasure will be yours, Meg,' she'd said. Meg had wanted to ask where she was going, but it didn't seem polite. She'd been told often enough not to question adults, but then there were so many things she needed to know.

Mrs Watson seldom went out and, when she did, it was nearly always to the cinema or 'pictures' as she called it. A long time ago the late Mr Watson had played the piano in a picture house that showed silent movies and Mrs Watson had often accompanied her husband on these occasions. Meg loved to hear her talk about the films they had seen: how they had laughed at a man with a funny walk called Charlie Chaplin and how she had been terrified when someone called Pearl was tied to a railway line minutes before a train was due. Mr Watson had had to play the piano very loud and very fast for that bit.

'We all knew that Pearl would get free just in time,' the old lady said, smiling, 'but we pretended we didn't. We used to have such fun at the pictures in those days.'

Now, although Mrs Watson lived on her own, she still went to the cinema as often as she could and always sat near the front like she had in the days of the silent movies. Meg knew there was a special film that the old lady had been waiting to see for ages and, looking through the gate on that particular day in August, Meg hoped she would see Mrs Watson striding down the street in her brown coat and hat on her way to catch the bus to the pictures.

But somehow, in her heart of hearts, Meg realised that this would not now happen. There would be no more stories about the silent movies and her old friend would no longer be able to give her the promised treasure. Mrs Watson had been wrong. There wasn't always plenty of time.

The first heavy air raids causing casualties in Coventry began in August 1940.

The Rex Cinema was showing the film Gone With The Wind when it was destroyed on Sunday, 25th August.

Chapter 9

'We are sure that in the end all will be well.'

Winston Churchill

The summer came and went without anyone really noticing the weather.

During August the Battle of Britain was foremost in everyone's mind and, when Coventry itself began to suffer serious casualties from enemy air raids, people instinctively ceased to plan very far ahead. Families, realising that they would soon have to cope with some difficult times, concentrated on making their lives as normal as possible in the circumstances.

When the nights started to draw in and become colder, Meg's father made a hidey-hole under the stairs by reinforcing the walls. Blankets and pillows were left inside, so that the children could sometimes sleep there instead of always having to go down into the Anderson shelter. It was warm and a lot more comfortable than the shelter so Meg often slept there, fully dressed in her coat and wearing a pixie hood which her mother had knitted. Without her knowing, some of her father's ARP friends would sometimes call in just to look at Meg with her rosy cheeks, fast asleep and completely oblivious to what was happening outside.

John told Meg that it was now a 'real' war and that they were under siege. He decided that this meant that he needed to keep provisions in the hidey-hole 'just in case'. He wouldn't elaborate on what 'just in case' meant, but these provisions consisted mainly of a bottle of water and a tin of broken biscuits. One or two cups, badly cracked and lacking handles, were added later. Meg thought all this was very exciting.

In those days it was possible to buy bags of broken biscuits. The local Co-op stocked big square tins of different types of biscuits from which an assistant would weigh whatever a customer needed. The end tin contained broken biscuits from all the other varieties and were obviously much cheaper. John always made sure that his mother remembered to include some in her shopping for his provisions.

The Co-op provided a very reliable service throughout the war, despite the many problems it faced. Not only did Meg's mother shop at the local store for all their rations and other food but every morning the Co-op milkman delivered their allowance of two pints of milk on the doorstep. He seldom let them down, even after a heavy air raid when it meant parking his milk float where he could and walking the rest of the way. Meg's mother often said he was one of the unsung heroes of the war.

Meg took a few treasures of her own with her when she went under the stairs: the doll with the fixed eyes, an old colouring book with a few crayons and *Sunny Stories* by Enid Blyton. This last treasure was there in the hope that her brother would read to her, which he did occasionally. Sometimes he made up his own stories or told her about things that he himself found interesting, especially anything that was mechanical.

It was John who first explained to Meg what the sound of the sirens stood for. He told her that the wailing sound meant that enemy aircraft had been sighted coming this way and everyone needed to take cover. The siren that sounded a single note at the end of an air raid was originally called the 'Raiders Passed' signal. The name 'All Clear' had previously been intended to signal, if necessary, the end of a gas attack informing everyone that the air was clear again.

John never went anywhere without his copy of the Penguin *Aircraft Spotters Manual*. He showed Meg the pictures of the allied planes and taught her to recognise the sounds made by the engines of different aircrafts. It wasn't difficult even for a little girl to recognise the heavy, uneven chugging noise made by the German bombers as they flew overhead. It was a sound Meg soon grew to fear.

The children were losing a lot of sleep because of the frequent warning sirens, so their mother would sometimes leave them in bed until it became obvious that a raid really was about to happen.

One night she left it too late. Before she could get Meg dressed, a bomb exploded on to the houses at the back, causing all the windows to shatter. A shower of broken glass invaded the room. Meg was still standing on the bed at the time and her mother hit her hard with her arm, so that her daughter fell on to the floor just as an enormous piece of shrapnel embedded itself in the wall behind where her head had been. Meg had been saved from a very serious injury, if not worse, and she promptly burst into tears.

One of the houses that had been hit was the home of a friend Meg had made since Tom no longer came to visit. The whole family had been in their shelter when the bomb struck and, although their home was destroyed, they weren't injured. No one thought to tell Meg that her friend was unhurt until much later the next day and by then the incident, coming as it did on top of her own narrow escape, was stored in her memory. It was then that Meg first began to lose the sense of security that a small child needs.

By the end of October there was hardly anyone in the city who had not been personally affected by the ferocity of the air raids. The German pilots regularly flew in above the barrage balloons and out of reach of the searchlights which frantically criss-crossed the night sky. Occasionally one would make a daring daylight raid and strafe buildings and streets with gunfire.

One night, after a prolonged and heavy raid, some of the neighbours came out of their stuffy shelters to get some fresh air. They stood quietly in the back entry, a group of people in various stages of undress. In different circumstances they may not have had much in common, but now they took strength from each other's presence. It had been so hot shut inside their Anderson shelter that Meg was standing there, next to her brother, just in her nightdress and slippers. Soon she began to feel cold. Suddenly, out of nowhere, came the sound of a plane. It was flying so low that at first no one could tell the direction from which it was coming. By the time it appeared over the roof of Meg's home, it was already so close that they could all clearly see the swastika painted on its fuselage.

Not one person moved or even spoke.

The pilot had his canopy pushed back and, as the plane passed directly over the spot where Meg stood, his head appeared over the side and he looked down at them. She didn't feel the least bit frightened. Somehow she knew that he wouldn't hurt them.

John said later that the pilot had been roof hopping in order to avoid the beams from the searchlights as he tried to get back home. He wouldn't have known that he was flying into the range of the anti-aircraft guns that were stationed on the railway sidings, and they never knew whether he made it back to base or not.

After another air raid, which caused the recently replaced windows to shatter again, Meg went with her mother to buy some more curtain material. She knew her father thought it was a rather pointless thing to do in the face of increasing air attacks, but her mother was becoming very insistent that the house should be neat and tidy at all times, not in spite of the war, but because of it. So once again she put a protesting Meg into the old pushchair and struggled with it over all the debris into town.

Up the Morris Hill they went and across Broadgate towards Trinity Street. Trinity Street with its wide road and new shops had only been constructed just before the war in 1937 so it was still a popular area for visitors.

Once more they were met by scenes of devastation. Owen Owen's, where Meg's mother had hoped to buy the curtain material, had taken a direct hit. A woman who came over and spoke to them was in tears. She said that this damage was nothing compared to the fact that Ford's Hospital, the lovely old almshouses, had also been destroyed and the matron with some of the elderly lady residents had been killed.

On hearing this, Meg's mother, without any shopping and without saying another word, turned the pushchair round and went home.

'Swastika' originated from the Sanskrit word for prosperity and was officially adopted as the emblem of Nazi Germany in 1935. It had been an ancient good luck symbol.

The word 'strafe' comes from a German First World War catchphrase, 'Gott strafen England!' ('May God punish England!')

Chapter 10

'The sun has got his hat on
Hip, hip, hip, hooray
The sun has got his hat on
And he's coming out today.'

A song to skip to

By now there wasn't a single aspect of life that wasn't affected by the war. No longer did anyone think things would soon get back to normal. In some ways it was a relief not to have to pretend any more. It was a question of living one day at a time and making the best of that particular day.

Coventry kids became very good at this. The bombed buildings quickly became their playgrounds. This was of course strictly forbidden and, unfortunately, nasty accidents did take place. One of John's friends was injured when a den, which the boys had been building on a bombsite, collapsed on top of him. Later one of Meg's first school friends lost a leg when she was buried by a wall that collapsed as she was leaning against it.

Without toys to play with and without supervision by adults, who were weighed down by the problems of day-to-day living, children were left to amuse themselves. They were, needless to say, very resilient.

Even after a difficult night and without much sleep, the older ones would be up early next morning collecting shrapnel. Meg joined in with this, but rather naively she would store the pieces she'd found in the bottom of her toy cupboard and her mother kept throwing them away. John, being that much older and supposedly wiser, hid his collection in a hole in the garden.

There were some games that boys and girls often played together. One of these was Five Stones. It was popular because it was so easy then to find five stones of roughly the same size and it could be played anywhere, indoors or out. Some children became very skilled at this game and threw the stones up quite high before catching them on the backs of their hands. Meg, having small hands, usually only managed to catch one or two stones at a time and sometimes caught none at all.

However she, like many other small children, soon learned not to get upset. If they wanted to be part of the gang they had to play by the same rules as everyone else and, anyway, after a couple of years or so they were no longer the smallest members in the group and then they too could show off their talents.

Skipping was very popular with girls as it could be played with any number of players and it was fairly easy to find a piece of thin rope in someone's shed. After petrol was rationed, there was very little traffic on the residential roads which meant that two girls holding a long skipping rope at either end could stretch it across the full width of the street while the others could all skip together. Meg gradually became involved in the highly competitive skipping games that were devised for both singles and teams, and she became quite an expert.

Various forms of hopscotch were also popular. The children could use pieces of white plaster taken from the inside walls of bomb-damaged houses as a substitute for pieces of chalk. It was easy to use the existing paving slaps for traditional hopscotch but, when that started to become boring, the players chalked more complicated circular versions of the game in the middle of the road – hopping on one leg back on to the pavement if a car did happen to come along.

John and his friends became adept at searching through badly bombed buildings for anything that could be useful. Looting itself was a serious offence, but these buildings were completely clear of personal belongings and were just empty shells waiting for the demolition men to finish the job the enemy had started.

Meg's father made a cricket bat from an old floorboard, which John had found in one of these houses. A ball was made from circular strips cut from the inner tube of an old bicycle tyre. Starting with a small inner core, John and Meg painstakingly stretched the thin strips of rubber, doubled at first and then singularly, around the middle bit, criss-crossing until the last strip was difficult to put in place. Of course the resulting ball was very uneven, which made for some interesting bounces, but it was better than nothing.

The white plaster chalk was also used to draw a wicket on to the garden wall of a neighbour's house and someone's coat was used to mark the other end of the run. It was a popular after-school game on a summer evening and sometimes irritated the people who lived there, but they were usually very tolerant about it. Actually they owned the local fish and chip shop, a centre point of the local community, and knew most of the children as customers. This interested Meg more than the cricket. Towards the end of the war, when Meg was allowed to join the Brownies, she was sometimes given a three-penny bit by her father to buy a little bag of chips on her way home from the weekly meetings. As Meg and her friends walked happily along eating chips, she knew for certain that these were the best chips in the world.

Much to the disapproval of the adults, one of the games that the boys and some of the older girls played was called Rat-tat-ginger. In any row of houses, where two front doors were next to one another, two of the more agile youngsters would tie the door handles together with a thin piece of rope and knock both doors hard before running away. John, who was first a cub and then a scout, knew how to tie knots so he was often one of the main players in this game. Meg would watch him from a distance, as she couldn't run as fast as the others. They only allowed her to be there at all on the strict understanding that she told no one about it. She wouldn't have done anyway as she was much too worried about what would happen if anyone found out that John was involved. They'd got into terrible trouble once when they'd been caught scrumping apples because she hadn't been able to climb back over the wall fast enough.

In the natural order of things, these sort of activities tended to fade away as the bombing increased and the older children started to be evacuated. Stamp collecting and writing to pen friends became popular as these could take place indoors. Good books became more scarce to buy, so on Saturday mornings many children would go to the library in Kingsway and try and find a Biggles book or something by Enid Blyton that they hadn't already read. Angela Brazil was popular as a writer of school stories for girls. Meg was very surprised years later when she found out that Angela Brazil's family had lived in Coventry at No 1, the Quadrant.

Once, during the school holidays, a small group of local children put on a concert in Meg's garden. The 'stage' was the area outside the back door and an old curtain, hanging from a piece of rope tied between the fence and the coalhouse, provided the backdrop. Some of the children sang and danced, some performed acrobatics, but the star turn was a surprise appearance by John. Dressed in an oversize jacket of his father's and an old button cap, he sang:

> 'I've got a sixpence – jolly, jolly sixpence
> I've got sixpence to last me all my life
> I've got tuppence to spend
> And tuppence to lend
> And tuppence to take home to my wife.'

Then he did a little jig and sang the verse again.

It may have only been a brief performance, but the fact that John had put in an appearance at all was significant. His father, by then realising that his son would have to grow into an adult without the benefit of a normal boyhood, had taken to spending some more time with him. This was beginning to have unexpected results. John had begun to show more tolerance, helping Meg when she needed it and doing odd jobs for his mother without being asked. It was his father who had secretly groomed John for the unexpected appearance at the concert.

They had obviously reached some sort of understanding. When the new season started, he began taking his son to the Saturday football matches at Highfield Road, having been a Coventry City supporter for most of his life. To say that John enjoyed these outings was an understatement. On the days that City was playing at home, he would be up early, whatever the weather, being especially helpful to his mother and making absolutely certain that nothing could stand in the way of his attending the game.

It wasn't far to Highfield Road from where they lived. On match days men and a few women would walk from all over the city along the roads leading to the ground. 'Streams of coats and caps,' Meg's mother said. She would leave the back door open and they would be able to tell the progress of the game just by listening to the noise coming from the crowd. Without much traffic around the sound carried a long way. What usually started as a low rumbling would gradually increase in volume until the roar broke into a crescendo and Meg's mother would say, 'City's scored!' At other times the noise subsided into a drawn out groan and she just said, 'Oh dear.' Every so often there would be the sound of polite clapping, which meant that the other side was playing well, and if they scored – well that was quite difficult to judge.

It was usually possible, as the afternoon progressed, for Meg to guess what sort of mood her father and brother would be in when they returned home – enthusiastic or subdued. She loved it when they were really happy. Her mother would try and make sure she had something nice ready for tea and they would sit around the table, laughing and joking.

Later, when far away from home feeling lonely and miserable, Meg would try and think about moments like these.

There was a time she would always remember. One Saturday afternoon, after her father and John had gone to watch the football match between Coventry City and Reading, the warning siren sounded. Meg's mother called her indoors from the garden and, for a while, they sat under the stairs, worrying whether the others would manage to get home or find a shelter somewhere. When nothing seemed to be happening, Meg's mother tentatively left the hidey-hole and was amazed to hear the sound of the crowd roaring from Highfield Road. It was some time before the All Clear sounded.

When the football supporters eventually started drifting back towards the town, John ran in, highly excited. He said that when the siren had sounded the referee was about to stop the match, but it was at a crucial moment and the spectators demonstrated against the decision so he conferred with both captains and allowed play to continue.

His father was smiling broadly when John had finished speaking. He looked across at his wife and said, 'We were all winners today, Luv.'

During difficult times, Coventry City football team and the Highfield Road ground provided a welcome source of stability for many Coventrians.

On Friday, 15th November 1940, the day after the Coventry Blitz, **The Midland Daily Telegraph** *managed to produce a two-page (four sides) newspaper. Although it was full of the terrible happenings of the previous night, the football fixture list for the next day was still in its usual place on the back page. Coventry City had been down to play West Bromwich Albion at home. Kick off at 3.00 pm.*

Chapter 11

'Man's inhumanity to man Makes countless thousands mourn.'

Robert Burns

The night of Thursday, 14th November 1940 was cold, very cold. It was also very clear with a full moon, which made some people uneasy. Moonlight was not romantic during the war – it was something to be feared.

Meg's father mentioned during tea that he had noticed some oil containers with chimneys lining one or two of the roads on the outskirts of town. These were supposed to be able to provide a smokescreen for Coventry against attacks. He smiled, saying he didn't think they would be very effective against planes which often dropped flares to light up targets before a raid.

That evening the sirens sounded and, once again, German aircraft began passing overhead. Although Meg's father wasn't officially on duty that night, he quickly bundled the two children under the stairs before grabbing his tin hat and running out.

Almost immediately incendiary bombs started raining down on the city, creating fires which guided the bombers to their targets. Meg's mother thought she would be able to put a fire out if she had enough water, so she called to John to help her fill any containers he could find while she stood outside the back door ready to defend their home at any price.

Meg had put on her coat and pixie hood and stood cowering in the doorway leading to the hidey-hole. This was already worse than anything she could have imagined. The pounding of the guns was incessant, the noise overwhelming. Meg wanted it all to stop. She put her hands over her ears but couldn't make the noise go away. Suddenly her father came running back into the house, calling for her mother to leave everything and get the children. He didn't want them to go into the Anderson shelter by themselves, so he took them to a communal shelter over the road.

The only thing Meg's mother had managed to pick up as they left the house was her handbag. Since the beginning of the war, she had kept to the habit of leaving her bag on the hall table so that she never left home without it. It held their most important documents: birth certificates, identity cards, bank books, ration books and the housekeeping money.

Meg had just her doll and John his emergency rations – a bottle of water and some broken biscuits. As they ran over the road, it seemed as if the sky itself was on fire, so bright was the glow from the burning city. But when they reached the safety of the shelter, the warden standing at the entrance shook his head at Meg's father and said, 'Sorry, mate. There's no more room here – not an inch of space left. You'll be more comfortable using the shelter in the garden next door.'

As they turned to go he touched Meg's father on the arm. 'Good luck, mate.'

Her father leaned back towards the man and shook his hand. 'You too. We'll have a drink when it's all over.'

The man grinned. 'We will,' he said. 'We certainly will.'

The shelter they were told to go to was the one at the end of Mrs Watson's garden. It hadn't been used since her house had been destroyed and was cold and damp. It was also dark and Meg didn't like it at all. There was just a plank laid across some bricks to sit on. Her father's torch did nothing to dispel the gloom and he told her mother he would go back to their house for some candles. She looked at him anxiously but just nodded. It seemed ages before he returned, but when he came back he was carrying a blanket and two cushions. He gave John the torch to hold and took some candles and a box of matches from one of his coat pockets and some apples from the other.

'I had some trouble finding anything,' he said to Meg's mother. 'There's no electricity. I'm going back in a moment to make sure we shall still have some water to use in the morning. The mains could be damaged as well by then.' He looked at his son for a moment. 'It would help if John came with me to hold the torch,' he said.

Meg's mother started to protest, but John had already got up to leave. He hadn't spoken since they had left home. Being some years older than Meg, he already knew that what was happening that night was different from anything they had experienced before. Bombs were being dropped at the rate of one every two minutes and the anti-aircraft guns, placed around the city, pounded continuously. It was a desperate situation. The sheer volume of noise made it almost impossible to communicate with one another and John's father had to bend over him to speak in his ear. But John didn't need to be asked. He wanted to help in any way he could.

That night many boys had to do men's work. The communication system was wrecked early on so that boys, running and cycling where possible, were used as messengers. Some were injured. At least one was killed. But John didn't know that then. He just wanted to get out of that dismal shelter and help his father.

Without any other light except the small torch, getting the water took them some time, stumbling about in the dark to fill anything they could lay their hands on. Outside the moonlight, which would normally have been a blessing in the dark, meant that the bombers could find their targets more easily. Inside John's father double-checked so that not even the smallest chink of light from his torch could show through the blackout. It took them a long while to complete their task and, when they eventually went back over the road, it was to find two very worried looking faces peering up at them in the gloom.

At least they now had some more food and a bottle of milk to drink. John had brought some night lights in his pocket and, when these were lit, things became a little more cheerful. The light was still too poor to play many games so they sang some songs instead. Even Meg, who regularly listened to 'Workers' Playtime' with her mother could remember some of the words. Then her mother started singing her favourite song, 'The White Cliffs of Dover'. She very seldom sang, although she had quite a good voice, but she knew this one off by heart. When she reached the line 'And Jimmy will go to sleep in his own little room again,' she substituted the name 'Johnny' and leaned over and ruffled her son's hair. As her voice began to falter on the last line, their father joined in, 'There'll be bluebirds over the white cliffs of Dover, Tomorrow – just you wait and see.'

It was hard for Meg's parents to finish singing those words, knowing that, as they did, German bombers would be flying over those same White Cliffs on their way to attack an English town somewhere.

Just as Meg started to fall asleep, her father stood up. 'I'll have to go out for a while,' he said to her mother. 'I'll come back and look in on you when I can, but I can't sit here any longer. They're going to need every man they can get out there tonight.'

He wasn't usually a demonstrative man, but he bent down and kissed Meg and her mother awkwardly on top of their heads and patted John on his shoulder.

It was quiet in the shelter after he left. Though the three of them were exhausted, sleep now was out of the question. The bombardment seemed as if it would never stop. True to his word, Meg's father did manage to get back to see them. He didn't say what was happening outside, but even in the poor candlelight it was possible to see that, under the dust that covered most of him, his face was pale and drawn. He sat down on the plank seat and gulped down the milk that Meg's mother handed to him.

'You don't have to go out again, do you?' she said.

'Oh, I do…I am afraid I must,' he replied. Meg had never heard her father sound so shaken before.

Suddenly a whining noise came from overhead, increasing in volume as it got nearer.

'Oh my God!' he shouted. 'Down! Get down!'

Meg was sitting on her mother's lap at the time and he pushed them both on to the floor, pulling John with him as he fell down nearly on top of them. They all knew that something truly awful was about to happen. Just as it seemed the noise couldn't get any louder, the bomb exploded and everything came crashing in around them. The dust was choking them but her father managed to speak, telling them not to move. He began shouting for help but no one came. No one could hear above the noise that was still going on outside.

Meg lay there rigid with shock, the weight of her mother pressing her down on to the hard floor. She heard her father talking quietly and eventually felt herself able to move a little.

Then her mother spoke, breathing heavily. She told Meg, being the smallest, to crawl on her stomach to where the entrance to the shelter had been and not to stand up until she was well outside. Then she was to run as fast as she could to the communal shelter next door and tell them what had happened. All Meg could really remember later was the pain in her knees, as she wriggled through the debris towards the spot where the entrance had been, and seeing some men running towards the bombed shelter after she had spoken to them.

She never knew how long she stood just inside the communal shelter by herself. No one spoke to her, not even to enquire why she was there. Nothing was normal any more. When John appeared, she grasped his hand tightly and, for once, he didn't attempt to pull it away. He told her that their father had taken their mother to hospital to have a wound in her head stitched. They were to stay where they were until the All Clear sounded and then go home.

'I have the front door key. We'll be all right,' he said.

Meg just nodded. They sat together on the sandbags at the entrance to the shelter, too shocked to speak and too tired even to move. As the times between explosions grew longer and the noise gradually abated, people came out of the shelter and leaned against the brick wall.

An ARP warden looked down at Meg and then knelt on the ground in front of her. 'I think we'd better get these cleaned up for you,' he said, gently touching her knees.

He pulled his canvas shoulder bag round in front of him and took out his first aid kit. It was only then that Meg realised that both her knees were bleeding.

On the night of 14th November 1940 the warning sirens sounded just after 7 pm. It was not until 6.16 am the next morning that the All Clear came. The Coventry Blitz had lasted for eleven hours non-stop.

The Nazis later claimed that this raid was the biggest single attack in the history of air warfare until then. Thirty thousand incendiaries were dropped to guide the bombers to their targets and German pilots reported seeing the glow of the fires in Coventry as they flew in over the coast.

Over five hundred planes dropped parachute mines and a thousand high explosive bombs.

Anti-aircraft guns situated around the city kept up such an attack that for a time some of the gunners were out of ammunition.

Streets became impassable, electricity was cut off, and gas, water and sewer pipes were shattered. Limited water for fire fighting was taken from the canal and the River Sherbourne. Soon after this raid, static water tanks were placed around the city.

That night in Coventry five hundred and sixty-eight people were thought to have been killed and one thousand and two hundred people injured.

On 14th November 1940 a new word entered the German language: 'Coventrieren'. In English: 'Coventrate'. Its meaning – to lay waste by aerial bombardment.

Chapter 12

'The people of Coventry bore their ordeal with great courage.'

Official communiqué

When the warden told them it was all right to do so, Meg and John returned home. The acrid smell of smoke and dust hung heavy in the air, but dawn was slowly creeping over the fires still raging in the city.

As John opened the front door it was obvious that no one was there. The house was dark and cold and just a few glowing embers remained in the grate. He took the remaining candle stubs from his pocket and lit them before placing them in a row on the hall table.

'We can open the blackout curtains in a moment,' he said to Meg, who was standing silently in the hall with tears running down her face.

'Come on,' he said, but not unkindly. 'We've got to get the fire going before Mum and Dad come back, and then we can boil up a kettle.'

Meg helped John pull the curtains back and then collected some small pieces of coal and wood from the bottom of the scuttle. Her brother placed these on the fire, bit by bit. Fortunately the grate was still quite hot and, after blowing a few times, he managed to get the embers going. There was no electricity, gas or water. Their father had been right. John filled the kettle with water from one of the containers left ready and placed it on the stand that fitted over the front of the fire.

All the time he was thinking of little things for Meg to do. 'There, we'll soon have a cup of tea,' he said, subconsciously mimicking his mother. Telling Meg to call him if the kettle started to boil, John went into the kitchen, carefully washed his hands in a little of the water in the sink and got the teapot and cups from the cupboard. Just then came the sound of the front door being opened and their parents walked in.

Meg's mother had a bandage around her head and over one eye, but she was still able to smile at her two children, relieved beyond words to see them both safe and for them all to be back together in their own home. Meg's father lifted Meg up and put his free arm around John's shoulder as the boy buried his head in his father's jacket.

'It's been a long night for you, son,' their father said. 'It's been a long night for both you and Meg.' He was so proud of his children, and the cup of tea, which was quickly pressed into his hand, although tasting very weak, was the best cup of tea he had ever had in his life.

Meg's mother soon went upstairs to lie down. Meg's father sat down with his daughter on his knee and asked what had happened to them both. Meg proudly showed him her bandaged legs and John told him how they had returned home together after the raids had stopped. Their father listened, nodding every so often to show he was listening. He couldn't find the right words to say. He knew that his family had escaped death by a hair's breadth that night. If they had been sitting on the other side of the shelter, they would have been crushed. The concrete roof had collapsed at an angle to rest on top of a pile of bricks on their side, and it was this that had saved them. It was a miracle that they had all survived with so little injury. But for him to leave his children under those conditions, while he took his injured wife to hospital, was a decision no man should ever have to take. On that night people had to fend for themselves as the city became the centre of many terrible incidents. It was a relief that the children had not witnessed any of these.

The nearby pub, where Meg's father sometimes met his ARP colleagues after work, had received a direct hit. Some of the customers, who had taken refuge in the cellar, had been killed instantly and more had been injured. As he helped his wife past the bombed building, he saw men and women clawing desperately at the rubble with bare hands, trying to find relatives and friends who might still be trapped.

When Meg's parents finally reached the hospital they were confronted by an unforgettable sight. Hundreds of casualties were being brought in and, as there were not enough beds or chairs, they lay or sat on the floor until they could be treated by one of the exhausted staff. Every so often a nurse would shake her head and someone would be quickly removed elsewhere.

It was a long time before anyone could attend to Meg's mother. By then, anaesthetic was in short supply and a very tired lady doctor apologised for the fact that she would have to stitch up the wound without using any pain relief. At that moment a man walked through the hospital door carrying his small daughter who had lost most of one leg. After that, having her wound stitched without anaesthetic was not important to Meg's mother.

Neither of Meg's parents spoke about what they had seen that night until many years after the war, but the images could never be erased.

Like so many others, the trauma of the Coventry Blitz was to remain with them for the rest of their lives.

The Aftermath

'Father forgive!'

On Thursday, 14th November 1940 a famous Midlander was buried. Neville Chamberlain, whose policy of appeasement had failed to prevent the outbreak of World War II, was quietly laid to rest in Westminster Abbey. Officially there were no flowers, at his own request, but by the side of his coffin lay a heart-shaped wreath of orchids from his native city of Birmingham.

That very night the Germans, whom he had sought to appease, tried hard to annihilate another famous Midland city. The next day they knew that, although they may have destroyed many ancient buildings in the heart of Coventry, they hadn't succeeded in breaking the spirit of its people.

On Friday, 15th November the citizens of Coventry started to resurrect their stricken town. They found that over sixty thousand houses had been damaged and only a few of the city centre buildings remained intact. But, even though they had gone without sleep for over twenty-four hours and there was no transport, many people made their own way into town. Some were indignant when stopped from trying to get through to their places of work, even though most of these no longer existed. Others just waited quietly at the Council House for news of relatives and friends. Hundreds stayed to help with the task of clearing up. It was a mammoth job.

There was not enough water to quench the fires and some of these continued to burn throughout the day.

The lovely old Cathedral of St Michael's was reduced to a shell. Only its stark walls and the smoke-blackened steeple remained standing, but on top of the still smouldering rubble lay two charred beams – in the shape of a cross.

The Provost received a huge number of letters of sympathy from across the world. Aid was sent to Coventry by both the rich and the poor, often from other cities that had also suffered, such as London and Birmingham. People just wanted to help, like the Liverpool family who sent the money they had been saving for Christmas – £2.10s (£2.50).

The following message was wired from HMS Coventry: *'The complement of HMS* Coventry *expresses sympathy with the citizens in their adversity and assures them that the ship will endeavour to repay.' Sadly many of the crew, some of them from the city, repaid with their lives. On 14th September 1942 HMS* Coventry *was sunk off Tobruk. It was reported that the proud ship went down with her colours still flying.*

On Saturday, 16th November 1940 King George VI, a tall, thin man in a military great coat, visited Coventry at his own request and walked around the town talking to its people for hours.

The November Blitz on Coventry helped to influence American opinion regarding the war. Among many articles which appeared in their newspapers during the following days were:

The New York Times
'If the destruction of Coventry awakens our people to a new sense of Britain's danger, the victims of this horror will not have died in vain.'

The St Louis Globe Democrat

'The smouldering ruins of Coventry are new evidence that the Nazi war machine has stripped the last tenuous shred of civilisation from modern warfare.'

The Cleveland Plain Dealer

'Hitler raises horror to the superlative. There is not enough room in the twentieth century world for the author of Coventry's sorrow and for decent man at the same time.'

The New York Tribune

'The gaunt ruins of St Michael's Cathedral, Coventry, stare from the photographs, the voiceless symbol of the insane, the unfathomable barbarity which has been released on Western civilisation. No means of defence which the United States can place in British hands should be withheld.'

Within a few days of the bombing, one thousand and five hundred men from the forces were sent to the city to clear the debris and make properties safe. Food rationing was temporarily suspended for two weeks but, until the power was restored, many people were forced to cook meals and boil water and milk on open fires. Because of the damaged sewers the Ministry of Health also offered inoculation against typhoid. People shared accommodation and coped. Everything possible was done to get things moving again.

Within four weeks some production was resumed in repaired factories, and transport was borrowed from other towns. Buses from Blackpool drove around the cleared areas displaying their seaside livery. The city was back in business.

But the city also had to care for its dead and Coventry became one of the first places in Britain, during the Second World War, to hold mass funerals and bury many of its dead in a communal grave. Apart from the victims of the November Blitz, the two heavy raids that the city suffered the following Easter meant another three hundred people were given a mass funeral. Churchill visited the city's communal grave at Coventry Cemetery in the summer of 1941.

After the war ended, a walled garden memorial was created at the cemetery and eight hundred and eight names carved into the stone monument, the last one being 'an unknown soldier of the 1939–1945 war'. The dedication on the centre of the memorial ends with the words of the twenty-third Psalm:

*'Though I walk through the valley
of the shadow of death, I will
fear no evil for Thou art with me.'*

Chapter 13

'Colds spread in crowded shelters – TAKE VICK WITH YOU.'

1940s advertisement

It was another cold and snowy winter. To Meg it seemed that she would never be free of the chilblains which irritated ever single one of her toes. Her hands were chapped and the tops of her legs, between the horrible, itchy woollen stockings and her liberty bodice, were always red and sore.

Every time the warning siren sounded there was the difficult decision to make between going down to the garden to the damp shelter or running the risk of staying under the stairs. Freezing nights meant that the family, more often than not, remained in the house.

During the early spring Meg began having difficulties in swallowing. No one was very concerned about this as most people were suffering from health problems in one way or another. The harsh conditions many were living under meant that colds and sore throats were common. Then Meg started having breathing problems as well. At first it was thought to be tonsillitis but, when the doctor insisted that she went into hospital, it was discovered that she had diphtheria.

Outside the raids continued but Meg was now suffering in her own little world. She had no recollection of how she'd arrived at the hospital and normal life ceased to exist for a time. The small, bare room she found herself lying in had a single bulb hanging from the ceiling, though there was not enough light to give her any comfort. Meg's throat hurt too much to cry. When she eventually became more aware of what was happening around her, the city was again under attack from the air.

It was the week before Easter 1941.

On Tuesday, 8th April the warning alert sounded just after 9 pm and Meg once again heard the familiar noise of enemy planes flying overhead. The curtain hanging over the tiny window in her room couldn't completely block out the eerie red glow from the fires already burning in the city and Meg closed her eyes and turned her face to the wall. She had never felt so frightened and alone in her life. She could just make out the sound of running footsteps in the corridor outside. The bare light bulb swung frantically to and fro until it finally gave out altogether and Meg was left lying in the dark.

The next moment she found herself being lifted out of bed and carried to safety under the red cloak of a nurse. Meg was very thin at this time and, as the nurse ran out of the building, her body was gripped so tightly that it was painful. She had become used to pain, but she would never become used to air raids.

The hospital at Whitley, to which Meg was transferred, was a forbidding place in the war years for a child. She found it difficult to cope with the strict regime of an isolation hospital and it seemed to her that nobody was at all friendly. The matron came round to inspect the wards every morning and only spoke if she found something wrong. This was more to do with the way the beds had been made than the small patients in them.

The rules were severe and never broken. The only way Meg saw her parents was through the taped-up glass of the windows. Not only were they not allowed into the ward but they couldn't give anything directly to her either. All sweets had to be handed to one of the staff so that they could be shared between all the children. Meg realised that she wasn't getting most of the sweets her mother showed her through the window and, although she must have been given sweets intended for other patients, Meg didn't understand this at the time. It was minor incidents such as this that Meg focused on. She tried not to think about the things which upset her the most.

Meg became unhappy and run down and her recovery was slow. She picked up other infections, which meant her stay in hospital had to be extended by many weeks. She was still too young, however, to realise that she also had a raw-looking red scar across her throat, the result of a hurried tracheotomy operation that had saved her life.

Then at long last something nice happened for Meg. A young nurse arrived in the children's ward. She was small, plump and cheerful. More importantly she actually liked the children in her care and they liked her in return. Within a few days of her arrival the young nurse had Meg out of bed, first sitting in a chair and then slowly walking up and down the ward, never pushing her, just allowing her to progress at her own pace.

When Meg became tired, the nurse would sit beside her curling the little girl's hair in rag strips. During the final weeks of Meg's stay in hospital, so much attention was paid to her blond hair that she went home looking like Shirley Temple. On that final day the young nurse waited with Meg until her mother arrived and then hugged and kissed the little girl as she left.

Meg had never felt so important before and, when she saw she was to travel home in a taxi for the first time in her life, she thought she would burst with happiness.

The Easter raids in 1941 were very severe and again caused serious loss of life and injuries in Coventry. Although the hospital had a huge red cross painted on the roof, it was hit on three consecutive nights. On the morning of Good Friday doctors, nurses and patients were found to be among the dead that once again Coventry had to bury. The victims were laid to rest with the others in the communal grave at the cemetery.

Many buildings were destroyed, including Christ Church, the Daimler, Courtauld's and the old Grammar School. The cities of Birmingham, London and Bristol also suffered loss of life and terrible damage on the same night.

Chapter 14

'The memories which stay with us longest are those we would wish to forget.'

The home Meg returned to from hospital was somehow different from the one she had left all those weeks before. It looked very much the same. Nothing had changed in the back room she was still sharing with her brother and she had peeped in the hidey-hole under the stairs to find the biscuit tin and water bottle still in place.

Nothing had actually altered but nothing felt the same. If Meg had been a few years older she would have realised that it was not the everyday things which had been affected but the atmosphere that had changed.

There were long silences in the house where once there had been conversations or music playing in the background. Her mother no longer bothered to switch on the wireless to listen to Alvar Liddell reading the news. If by chance the wireless happened to be switched on when the news started, she would often hurriedly turn it off. Meg's father no longer bothered looking after the flowers in the garden, but he still made sure they had some vegetables growing around the shelter as these were needed more than ever. Food supplies were sometimes scarce and Meg's mother complained constantly about the time she had to spend queuing at the shops. Having their own vegetables helped a great deal. But flowers were no longer important.

Even their visits to see Grandpa and Grandma were not pleasurable outings any more. The adults seemed only to talk about the war and Meg often sat by her grandmother without saying a word for the entire visit. She gradually began to comprehend that terrible things had been affecting the family while she had been in hospital and she listened carefully, trying to make sense out of these sombre conversations. One morning it became clear that something serious had recently happened to one of her uncles. Meg knew better than to interrupt with a question and she stayed quite still, as if this would help her understand better what had actually taken place.

Her uncle had been fire watching with another man on top of one of the factories in town when it had been bombed and both men had been reported missing, believed killed. As soon as Meg's grandfather heard the news, he went immediately to the factory site and questioned the men who were still searching among the ruins for survivors. He needed to know for certain what had happened to his son. He questioned everyone he could find, and a bystander who lived nearby told him that, although one of the men had definitely been killed, he had seen an ambulance taking someone else away on a stretcher. There was no easy way of finding out which hospital the casualty had been taken to so, without knowing whether it was his son or not, Meg's grandfather and other members of his family set about visiting every hospital in the area. As the only means of doing this was by cycling or walking it took them two weeks before Meg's uncle was eventually found alive, although badly injured, at the Hospital of St Cross in Rugby.

It was on another occasion at her grandparents that Meg learned about one of her other uncles. He had also been going out whenever a raid was taking place. As a young man he had been disabled by a motorcycle accident and he believed that while other men were away fighting he should do whatever he could at home. Sometimes this just meant cycling around the city acting as a messenger, but there were other times when he became involved in incidents so distressing that he was unable to talk about them.

By far the most tragic of these occurred not far from where he lived when he was with a group of men who tried frantically to rescue some women and children from a burning cellar. This was situated under an elastic factory and being used as an air-raid shelter. When the factory was hit, the stored rubber turned it into a fireball. Meg's uncle never fully recovered from the scene that faced him and the other men who finally managed to enter the building. He could never accept the fact that so many women and small children had suffered such a horrible death.

During the war in Britain more than seven thousand and five hundred children under the age of sixteen were killed during bombing raids in Britain. A similar number were seriously injured.

Many other young children involved in bombing incidents grew up with fears and anxieties that resurfaced in later life and were difficult to deal with.

Chapter 15

'Operation Pied Piper'

Official name for the evacuation procedure

Since her return from hospital, Meg's brother, John, had become very quiet and withdrawn. He no longer told Meg stories at night in bed, nor did he try to help her as much as he used to. But he wasn't cross with her when she did something wrong either. It was if he didn't care much any longer. Meg didn't know what she'd done wrong, but she would have preferred him to shout at her from time to time.

Then one day, when she asked him to help button up her cardigan, he just shook his head and said, 'You're going to have to learn how to do all these things yourself, Meg.'

She frowned at him a little, not saying anything. He waited as she struggled until all the tiny buttons were in the correct holes.

'We're going to be sent away, you and me.'

'On holiday?' She brightened up. They had all gone to Llandudno for a few days after her stay in hospital and she'd liked that very much.

'No. We're not going on holiday. We're going to be evacuated. Not Mum and Dad. Just you and me.' With that, he walked out of the room.

It was the first time Meg had heard the word 'evacuated' but she just knew it was horrible. It sounded horrible and if John didn't like it then neither did she.

Since being ill and away from home for all that time Meg had grown a little more confident. It wasn't that she was less afraid of the consequences of her actions, just that she was more insistent that her voice should be heard. She no longer remained in the background waiting until she was told about everything. Now she asked and kept on asking until she received an answer. This new stance of hers was not always well received but it usually had the desired effect, so off she went to find her mother to tell her she didn't want to be evacuated, whatever it was.

This time it didn't work so well. Her mother shouted at her and then at John, because he had told Meg about it when he shouldn't have, and then John shouted at them both before storming out once more. Meg was sent to bed early that night, none the wiser, but knowing for certain that evacuation must be a very terrible thing indeed for it to cause all this trouble.

Despite the children's protests, the parents decided that they had no choice but to evacuate the two children – there were still threats of more air raids. So on an early summer day in 1941, John and Meg were driven to a farmhouse near a village they had never even heard of and left with people they had never met before.

If it was a shock for John and Meg, it was also a shock for the farmer and his wife who had no children of their own. They saw a defiant young boy wearing grey shorts, black blazer and his school cap and with a hostile look on his face. His little sister, who was clinging to his hand, looked completely overwhelmed and close to tears. Her gas mask in its cardboard box hung limply on the string round her neck and her nametag was already completely crumpled. The farmer's wife immediately took pity on them both, leading the way indoors to the big farmhouse kitchen, where she handed them each a mug of tea and a slice of cake.

In many ways John and Meg had a better start to being evacuated than many other children. Although the house was rather gloomy with dark furniture and cold stone flags on the floor, the land around it became one big playground and, being summer, they made the most of it.

The farm buildings were on a hill that sloped gently down to a narrow stream. It was only a shallow piece of water, so Meg often took her sandals and socks off to collect the watercress that grew under its banks. There was a little wooden footbridge leading over the stream to the field on the other side and in the spring this field would look yellow from the mass of cowslips that grew in the grass. Meg had never seen these lovely wild flowers before and spent many happy afternoons sitting in their midst making chains from the daisies which grew among them. Looking back on that time, Meg always recalled cowslips as being tall flowers and when she eventually saw them again, many years later, she was surprised that they weren't so tall after all.

The happiest days Meg spent on the farm were at harvest time, when the whole place seemed to come alive. Extra hands had to be taken on to help with the harvest and these men, unlike the reserved farmer and his wife, would make a fuss of the children, throwing Meg on to the bales of hay and lifting her on to the old cart horse for a ride after it had finished its work in the fields.

But country life wasn't always so happy. It had its bleak side, as Meg was soon to discover. One of the tasks she had been given to do was collecting the eggs every morning from the hencoops that were dotted about the field over the stream. She really loved this job. She took the basket, which had a protective layer of straw at the bottom, and carefully lifted the warm eggs from each coop before gently placing them in the basket. Meg got to know all the hens individually and gave them names. She liked to think that they recognised her when she visited their homes.

One autumn morning, however, the farmer stopped her from going into the field. During the early hours many of the hens had been attacked by a family of foxes. They had managed to break through the rather old and rotting wood of the coops. Some of the hens had only their heads bitten off and the bodies had been left in a tangled mess of blood and feathers. Meg saw all this from the other side of the stream and cried. She didn't cry in front of people very often; John had told her not to, but this was too much. The farmer was not an unkind man, but he didn't know how to deal with children. He patted Meg on the head and told her that it wasn't a good idea to give farm animals names. They weren't pets and it often caused unhappiness when they were killed or sent off to market. He put all the remaining hens together in one of the barns close to the house where they would be safe and soon Meg had her first glimpse of the local hunt when it was invited on to the farmland to flush out the foxes.

Although during the summer months Meg had been quite happy playing around the farm on her own, as winter approached things changed. The countryside became less attractive and the farmhouse always seemed cold and gloomy. It had no electricity. At night oil lamps were lit in the main rooms and everyone had to carry candles with them to light the way. All the water had to be brought into the house from the well outside and used sparingly. Worst of all, the only lavatory was in a shed in the yard. It was really only a wooden seat over a bucket which had to be emptied regularly. The toilet paper was squares of newspaper strung together with string and doing this became another of Meg's responsibilities.

Meg felt alone and unhappy. John spent a lot of time at school even at weekends, so couldn't keep an eye on her and it became obvious that her health was again beginning to suffer. One day she was told that she would be going to school with her brother. After breakfast he waited while she got dressed in her warmest clothes and together in coats and wellington boots they walked across the fields to the village school. It had obviously been arranged especially to keep her happy. A place had been made for her in the infants' class and she had a little seat and table to herself at the side of the room. The teacher pinned Meg's name on her cardigan and gave her some paper to draw on with pencil stubs.

It was the best thing that could have happened for Meg at that time. She walked with John to school every morning and waited in the classroom for him at the end of the afternoon. There was an old-fashioned stove in the middle of the room and, although this was sometimes smoky, it meant that Meg always felt warm. She was the youngest and the smallest pupil in the school. Sometimes the teacher would beckon to her and, when Meg walked to the front of the class, she would pick her up and carry her around the desks while she talked to the other pupils.

For the whole of the time Meg was evacuated this teacher was the only person who ever showed her any affection.

The evacuation scheme started on 1st September 1939 – before war was actually declared. It was badly thought out and proved very traumatic for many of the children involved.

Where billeting was compulsory, it caused resentment as well as hardship. The children in many cases knew they were unwelcome.

To keep the evacuees occupied and away from the householders as much as possible, schools remained open longer for recreation activities. Teachers had to take their holidays in rotation to cope with the extra working hours.

None of this stopped a high proportion of the children from returning home. Happily on a local level, it was different and thousands of people were welcomed into Kenilworth, Leamington, Warwick and Stratford during the bombing.

Chapter 16

'We are all children of our environment – the good no less that the bad.'

Emily Lawless

Meg and her brother stayed on the farm for nearly a year. In all that time they only went back to Coventry once and that was for a few days at Christmas.

Although it wasn't the same as being at home, they both benefitted from the outdoor life and were always treated kindly.

Then, without warning and for reasons unknown to the children, the farmer and his wife moved and a new billet had to be found for Meg and John.

This time they were separated. John was invited to stay with the family of a friend he had made, but it was difficult to find a place for Meg and eventually the headmistress of the school reluctantly agreed to take her in until somewhere else was found.

The headmistress's house was attached to the school and this could have been good for Meg as she no longer had a long walk every morning. In fact it meant that she could never get away from the place where she soon began to be very unhappy. When Meg moved in, there were already two evacuees living in the house. They were quiet, timid girls, who were in the top class and would soon be moving to the big school where John was now a pupil. Meg never got to know them very well.

The headmistress had her sister living with her as a housekeeper, a situation which obviously suited them both, especially as one was forceful and very strict and the other was fearful and compliant. Having children in the house was something neither of them enjoyed, so they made sure their lives were disrupted as little as possible.

The girls were always given their tea as soon as classes finished for the day and then they sat at the kitchen table either doing their homework or reading until it was time for bed. The two other evacuees shared a bedroom and always went up the stairs together. Meg, who was in a small room by herself, felt very lonely and often cried at night when she was in bed and no one could hear her. Apart from school prayers every morning, the only time the three evacuees saw the headmistress was at the weekends. Then it was a rule that they all ate dinner together in the austere dining room. Except for grace, which was recited at the start, meals were expected to be consumed in absolute silence. Meg began to dread waking up on Saturday mornings knowing that she had to get through two whole days before school began again and her appetite started to be affected. Even though there wasn't a lot of it, she struggled to get through the food placed in front of her. She wasn't allowed to leave the table until every morsel had been eaten, so sometimes, long after the others had gone, she would wrap the remaining food in a bit of paper and smuggle it out, being careful to dispose of it without anyone noticing.

On Sundays everyone had to go to morning service at the church which was next to the school. Meg usually sat with the rest of the evacuee children in the back pews and this meant that she couldn't see anything but the people in front of her. She couldn't yet read well enough to be able to sing the hymns and only understood a little of what the vicar said. All she could do from where she sat was to look at the elaborately carved roof. Meg had once been told that, if she looked straight down the church aisle, she would be able to see that the roof curved slightly to the left. In medieval times this had been called a weeping chancel as it was said to depict the angle of Christ's head on the cross. Meg, of course, knew the Bible stories about the Crucifixion but, although she looked every Sunday, she still couldn't see anything different about the roof. The church always felt cold, even when the weather outside was warm and Meg soon began to dislike going there almost as much as she disliked being in the schoolhouse dining room.

One Sunday morning she woke up feeling particularly miserable and after breakfast told the headmistress that she didn't want to go to church that day. Meg knew that she would be shouted at but had not expected the reaction she received.

'You are a wicked, wicked girl,' the headmistress told her in front of everyone. Then she pulled Meg up the stairs by the ear and pushed her into her bedroom.

'If your parents come to visit this afternoon, you won't be able to see them now,' the headmistress added, vindictively. Then she locked the bedroom door behind her, leaving Meg in a state of terror.

Meg sat on her bed crying so much that she couldn't get her breath. After what seemed a very long time, she heard the key turn in the lock and, frightened that she was going to be punished again, pulled the eiderdown over her head. But the person who gently lifted the cover away was a young woman Meg had never seen before. She gave Meg a cup of warm milk and told her to try and drink some of it. Then she lifted Meg off the bed and took her downstairs.

When the others returned from church, they found a subdued Meg lying on the floor in the sitting room, colouring in a picture book. Nothing was said about the incident which had taken place and Meg, who had already been given some sandwiches by the young woman, wasn't ordered to go into dinner with everyone else. As it happened, her parents didn't visit that afternoon but her brother did, looking very upset. He stayed with her until quite late and the headmistress's sister gave them both some tea in the kitchen, which was most unusual. Meg never saw the young woman again, but John thought she was someone who had been working in the school.

Next day Meg went to lessons as normal, but within a week her mother had come to take her home.

It would have been nice if that could have been the end of her time as an evacuee but bombs were still falling on Coventry and a month later another billet had been found for Meg. Unfortunately, she was to be no happier there than she had been at the schoolhouse. Her new home turned out to be an old stone cottage, which actually backed on to the cowslip field in which Meg had spent many happy hours during her stay at the farm. There was a five-barred gate at the side of the cottage that led directly into this field.

The woman who lived at the cottage had sometimes helped out during the harvest and Meg remembered her smiling when the men had called her 'Little Miss Goldilocks'. When Meg and her mother walked up the path to meet her, the woman smiled again. But this time the smile did not reach her eyes. She didn't invite Meg's mother in for a cup of tea or ask her to stay awhile, so it was a very dejected little girl who was left waving goodbye on the doorstep still clutching her small case and gas mask.

Meg soon found out that, once again, she was not welcome. The woman told her that she had her own grandchildren from London staying at the cottage and there was no more room for another child. At night a small canvas bed was put up for Meg on the tiny landing, but this had to be taken down during the day as it was in everyone's way.

Perhaps it was understandable that the woman should feel hostile. Her life was hard enough already. She didn't need anything to make it worse. There was no sanitation of any sort. The lavatory was the same as at the farm – a bucket with a wooden seat over it – but in an even worse state, and all the washing had to be done in the sink after water had been brought in from the well outside. There was no electricity or gas, which meant that a fire had to be kept burning in the grate at all times, no matter how warm or cold it felt. There was not much money either. All these reasons must have influenced how the woman felt but none of them was the fault of any child.

If Meg had thought things were bad before, nothing had prepared her for this. She was expected to work before she went to school and then again at night. Some of the jobs she had to do were quite unsuitable for a little girl, but she had to do them just the same. The food she was given at mealtimes was sometimes different from that given to the other two children, who hardly ever spoke to her. In just a few days Meg began to look thin and dirty.

Again, John came to her rescue. One day, having heard through the evacuee children's network that his sister wasn't being well treated, he ran up the lane after school. When Meg saw him, she just clung to him so she didn't see the tears which came into his eyes when he saw how ill she looked. He gave her some sweets he had brought and told her she wasn't to worry any more. He would make sure they went home at the weekend whatever happened.

He was true to his word. Early on Saturday morning John arrived to fetch her. He helped her pack her few possessions in the small suitcase and made sure she had her gas mask with her. There was no one in the kitchen to see her go so, without saying goodbye, they let themselves out of the front door and walked up the lane to the main road.

It was a walk Meg had taken many times before, but she knew that this time would be the last. She thought of how often she had stood at the side of the main road, waiting for her parents to arrive on a visit and hoping that when they came they would take her back home with them. This day it would finally happen. So Meg sat patiently on the grass verge. Time was no longer a problem.

She saw that the gypsies had returned to the field on the corner. Their gaily coloured caravans stood in a circle around the campfire and their horses had been untethered so that they could graze at will.

Meg had seen the gypsies before when one day they had arrived at the farm to help bring in the harvest. At first she had been a little frightened of them, remembering how her mother reluctantly bought small sprigs of heather from women who knocked at the front door, looking different in their long skirts and shawls and often carrying a baby on their hips.

Now she was just intrigued by their carefree lifestyle and the children playing barefoot in the grass who seemed so much happier than any of the children she knew.

One of their mothers sat on the step of her caravan making wooden clothes pegs. When she glanced up and saw the little girl watching her, she walked to the five-barred gate and beckoned Meg to come over. With a smile, the dark-haired woman gave her a dolly peg and told her to keep it safe, as it would bring her good luck. Although Meg never knew whether to believe this or not, the peg was later carefully added to her small collection of treasures.

It was a long time before their parents arrived, but Meg waited happily sitting close to her brother.

Waiting was something she had learned to cope with. It was life in between the waits which was becoming more difficult.

More than one and a half million children were evacuated in Britain.

Although most of the evacuee children were treated fairly well in the circumstances, it was a difficult time for everyone involved. Billeting officers were appointed in all areas to keep an eye on everything, but people were being asked to take children into their homes without much warning or preparation and very little compensation. There was nothing orderly about the process. Children who had been living in towns with modern amenities often found themselves in rural areas without any amenities at all, while children from poor, inner-city slums were taken in by people who suddenly found themselves dealing with problems that often come with poverty.

Village schools were put under too much pressure, with staff and depleted supplies of material expected to cover a large increase in pupils and the rural idyll was often shattered by the unruly behaviour of some of the evacuees. It created animosity on both sides.

The surprise was not that evacuation didn't work too well, but that it worked at all.

Chapter 17

'Evacuation is a word best forgotten.'

When Meg returned home she was undernourished and had sores and boils on her body that took some time to heal. The doctor told her mother that, whatever was happening in the war, Meg must stay at home until she had fully recovered. He said that she was too young to withstand the continuing upheaval and needed reassurance and stability as much as anything else.

Meg's mother much admired the local doctor who lived nearby and held a surgery in the front room of his house. He had been a medical officer in the First World War until he was badly injured in Flanders. Although he now had an artificial leg, this never stopped him from going into blitzed homes during a raid to tend to the victims. On one particularly bad night an unexploded bomb landed at the back of his house. When an ARP warden tried to stop him from going back into his surgery, the doctor disregarded his advice, saying there was no point being a doctor if he couldn't have access to his medical supplies. His home was badly damaged so, the next day, he moved in with his sister and carried on looking after his patients as usual.

To Meg, the doctor, although always kind, seemed a rather remote person. Apart from his elderly sister, he had no family of his own and was rather reserved with children. But he would never accept any payment for treating a sick child. When Meg's mother once tried to remonstrate with him about this, the doctor told her that he could never refuse to treat a child just because the parents were unable to pay and, as some people were too proud to accept what they thought of as charity, he preferred to treat all children for free. He said his reward was to see them get better. He called in quite often to see Meg, until one day he declared her fully fit and said that she was in much better shape than he was.

It had been a warm summer, but the Midlands was still being subjected to air raids and the warning sirens sounded quite frequently. In June five enemy planes were brought down over Nuneaton and it was thought that Meg and her mother should stay with some family members in Leamington for a while. But this was only a temporary measure and soon Meg had to be evacuated once more.

John had already been back in his old billet for some time. He got on well with the people he was staying with and it was thought better that he should continue with his education without further interruption. Meg had to be found another place willing to take her in.

This time she went to a village not very far from Coventry so that her parents could visit her every weekend. This little place was already full with evacuees and the only people who agreed to have her were another pair of spinster sisters. One sister was the village nurse and the other was her housekeeper. They lived in a bungalow down a little lane near the church and Meg's mother was relieved to see that it had all the necessary amenities. Admittedly she was a bit concerned that Meg was to be the only child there, but thought that her daughter would soon make friends at school. Unfortunately, it wasn't as easy as that. Because all the other evacuees had been there for sometime, it was difficult for Meg to fit in. A main road divided the village in two and the only little girl she eventually got to know lived on the other side, so they didn't really meet very often after school.

Much like it had been before, the two middle-aged sisters were not very happy about having a child in their home and Meg spent a lot of time on her own. It was now autumn, a lovely time of the year in the country, and occasionally as a treat one of the sisters took Meg with her on visits to the big house. They were never invited in further than the kitchen, where cook would give Meg a glass of milk and a biscuit. It was always impressed upon her later how privileged she'd been to be invited into the big house, but Meg would have much preferred to see the rest of it. The nicest part of these visits was when Meg was told to run outside into the courtyard and collect some of the chestnuts which littered the drive. She loved doing this, especially when she was able to roast them back in the kitchen.

One day, as she and the sisters were walking through the churchyard, a young, smartly dressed woman wearing a fox fur came towards them. Meg's mother would have called her 'a swankpot'. She had a large Alsatian dog with her, which was off the lead, and as soon as it saw Meg it came bounding up, knocking her over on to the gravel path. Her knee was grazed quite badly and Meg cried but was told not to make such a fuss and pulled to her feet. The young woman, who apparently lived at the big house, was genuinely concerned and apologised profusely for the behaviour of the dog.

'I'm so sorry,' she said to Meg. 'He didn't mean to hurt you – he just wanted to play.'

Meg nodded tearfully at her and the lady gave her a little hug. She then tried to give her some money to buy some sweets, but Meg wasn't allowed to take it.

By the time she had got back to the bungalow and her knee cleaned and bandaged up rather roughly, Meg had almost been made to believe that it was her fault the dog had jumped up. 'Only babies cry,' she was told.

Whether that incident had anything to do with it, or whether it was an accumulation of all the events that had gone before, but that night Meg suddenly woke up and was violently sick. She was all right at school during the next day, but it happened again that night and the night after that. When her parents came at the weekend, they decided to take her home. This time she never went back.

It was some weeks before Meg totally recovered. The doctor told her mother that the trauma of continual night raids combined with the unhappy times she had gone through as an evacuee had been responsible for her illness. As he'd said before, she just needed to lead as normal a life as possible.

The air raids that took place that autumn over Coventry turned out to be the last the city had to suffer, so Meg never had to be evacuated again. It was not long before John returned home and in September both he and Meg were able to attend schools in Coventry. At last the children were able to experience some sort of routine which, pre-war, would have been taken for granted.

On Thursday, 3rd September, their mother insisted that they accompany her to the local church for the National Day of Prayer service, which had been organised to mark the day war had begun three years before. It was the first time Meg had been inside a church since she had been evacuated and she didn't enjoy the visit very much. However, in some ways, it became part of the healing process.

The last raids on Coventry were over Stoke Heath late in 1942.

On 26th August the King's brother, the Duke of Kent, was killed while flying on active service over Scotland.

Chapter 18

'Prisoners of war who bear their long exile with dignity and fortitude.'

King George VI (referring to British prisoners of war)

That September, as the war slipped into its fourth year, life for Meg began to settle down. She started going to the little school on the green, as her brother had done before her, and quickly made some new friends.

Clothes had been rationed since June 1941 so, to save coupons, her school uniform was made up of some new items mixed with others purchased through the school from previous pupils. Meg's mother refused to refer to them as 'second-hand clothes' but, as everyone else was in the same situation, it hardly mattered.

The streets of Coventry had, as far as possible, been cleared of rubble and this had left spaces and yawning chasms where once had been shops and office buildings. As the threat of air raids gradually diminished, the people walking about town began to look less worried and smiled more often. Soon the old familiar banter could be heard around the market stalls again.

Meg went into the market with her mother every Saturday morning. As a treat, they would, after shopping, go to the Geisha Café for a cup of tea and a biscuit. Occasionally it would be occupied by a group of American soldiers who joked and laughed all the time. Often they would good-naturedly tease the little girl about her blond curls while, at the same time, casting a surreptitious glance at her mother. Meg couldn't understand why some of the other people in the café frowned at the rather boisterous behaviour of these soldiers. 'GIs' they called them. She thought it was nice to see grown-ups having fun for a change. Many of the other men in uniform who came into the café looked tired and serious, particularly the Polish airmen who would sit there quietly, just talking to one another.

When she was older and able to understand more, Meg's father told her how hard it must have been for those men sitting in bomb-damaged Coventry, discussing what was happening to relatives and friends in their own war-torn country. It had been the same for British men who had returned from fighting overseas only to find that their families had suffered in bombing raids. The Americans never had that particular terrible worry so could appear to be more relaxed. Meg, of course, sympathised with the soldiers who had to cope with such distress. All the same she couldn't help giving a little smile whenever she recalled those GIs having fun ruffling a small girl's hair and slipping her packets of bubble gum when her mother wasn't looking.

The soldiers Meg did have difficulty dealing with were the German prisoners of war who had been brought into the area to mend the roads and carry out other necessary repair work around the town. At first she hadn't realised that these young men in their POW overalls with patches on the backs were the enemy until, that is, her mother told her that she was not on any account to speak to or even look at these men. She did of course look at them whenever she passed where they were working, but to her they bore absolutely no resemblance to the terrifying-looking men in helmets and jackboots who appeared in the Pathé newsreels at the Gaumont Cinema. These workmen just wanted to be accepted for what they were.

The war had taken too much out of the city for most adults to be able to accept prisoners of war as other than *the* enemy. When the mother of one of Meg's friends once invited a POW round to Sunday dinner, it caused quite a scandal.

Meg, herself, inadvertently became another source of gossip when she and a friend were discovered to be 'fraternising with the enemy'. This friend lived in a house with a garden backing on to some railway sidings. One day she told Meg she had a secret to show her over the wall at the bottom of the garden, but they had to be very careful not to be found out.

It was a struggle to climb on to the brick wall but they both finally made it. The view from the top was mainly of railway lines and trucks full of coal from the mines at Binley. However, there was also a young POW who was clearing the tracks along the embankment. When Meg's friend called to him, he looked around rather nervously and then came over to speak to them. His English was poor, but Meg's friend had obviously found a way of communicating with him and she gave him some sweets in a little bag that she took from her pocket. In return he passed them some German stamps.

Meg was thrilled. She was very careful to keep it a secret, just as her friend had impressed upon her, and they managed to climb on top of the wall two more times. But then one of her friend's neighbours had obviously seen them from an upstairs' window and lost no time in informing Meg's mother about what was happening. That was the end of it. Meg was punished quite severely but she had no regrets. She had already carefully stuck the stamps into her album without her mother knowing, and they remained in pride of place, an innocent symbol of a child's war.

The letters 'GI' stood for Government Issue (conforming to United States army regulations of standard government issue).

The ostracism of the German prisoners of war working in Coventry during the war was similar to the way townspeople treated the Royalist prisoners in the Civil War of the 1640s when the phrase 'sent to Coventry' originated.

In Europe some Allied POWs were treated harshly but others were able to lead a slightly more civilised existence, communicating with the outside world via the Red Cross. This included writing to and receiving letters from home and even taking various exams. In one interesting incident, which took place at the end of 1943, POWs were even able to purchase Rolex watches on an honour basis of buy now, pay later with invoices only becoming due when the war ended.

MONTRES ROLEX
SA
GENÈVE

SALES DEPARTMENT   TÉLÉPHONE : +41-22-308 22 00   3-7, RUE FRANÇOIS - DUSSAUD
                          TÉLÉFAX : +41-22-300 22 55   CH - 1211 GENÈVE 24

SW/jrf

20 July 2000

Dear

    Reference is made to your letter dated 16 July 2000 enquiring about Rolex watches delivered to prisoners-of-war in Germany during the 1940s.

    It is absolutely true that during the last years of the Second World War Rolex watches were sold to Allied POWs on an honour basis.

    The then Managing Director and founder of the Rolex Watch Company, Mr Hans Wilsdorf, sent watches to those Allied POWs in Germany, who were able to order them by mail, with invoices that only became due when the war ended.

    Several hundred watches were sent from Geneva and some 97% were paid for after the war. It is thought that the few watches that were not paid for never actually arrived and were either lost or stolen on the way.

    It is a tribute to human nature that this sort of deal could have functioned so well. Your friend should keep her husband's watch carefully for it really does have a story to tell.

    We remain,

                                                  Yours sincerely
                                          MONTRES ROLEX S.A.

BANGKOK BOMBAY BRUXELLES BUENOS AIRES CARACAS COLOGNE GENÈVE HONG-KONG JOHANNESBURG LONDRES MADRID MANILLE MELBOURNE MEXICO MILAN NEW YORK PARIS SÃO PAULO SINGAPOUR TAIPEI TOKYO TORONTO

Chapter 19

'In all our long history, we shall never see a greater day than this.'

Winston Churchill on VE Day

The last winter of the war began very much like the first – extremely cold with heavy snow blizzards in January. However it was followed by an abnormally warm February and March.

Although the war raged on in Europe and the Far East, Meg, happily making her way through the school, was now protected from its worst excesses.

She still carried her gas mask across her shoulders wherever she went, but this had become so much part of her life that she no longer really noticed it. She was certain that, come what may, she would never wear it. There had been two tests at school when they had all had to file into a mobile unit wearing their masks to see if they worked properly. As Meg could never breathe with hers on, she didn't see how it was ever going to benefit her during a gas attack. She just thought that, with or without it, she would be doomed. She liked to think she would die gracefully like the heroines in the books she kept reading, her last breath ending in a soft sigh. Fortunately Meg had never been told about the effects of gas poisoning.

The five long years had taken their toll on Meg's family, especially her mother. Coping with shortages had become an obsession and she kept repeating how difficult it was to find good food. The meat allowance wasn't enough to make decent meals for four people. Although Meg wasn't that bothered about food, she did enjoy the Sunday dinners when her mother had saved up enough coupons to buy a small piece of beef. Then they could have toast and dripping later on, when they all sat around the fire and listened to the wireless, toasting the bread on a long pronged fork in front of the glowing embers. Meg would often end up with a glowing face as well but she never minded that.

It was to be many years before food supplies got back to normal and rationing ended completely. Bread, for which Meg and her brother had to queue on Saturday mornings, wasn't actually rationed at all until *after* the war had ended.

Sweets were to remain on ration until 1953 and for John that was a real hardship. He and Meg would sometimes go to the chemist's and buy liquorice root, which they chewed, much to their mother's disgust. Other foods gradually returned. When sausages became available they contained such a high water content that they tended to burst in the pan if not pricked first, and everyone referred to them as 'bangers'.

It helped that the family still grew some vegetables in the garden and friends would often call in with surplus produce of their own. A sleepy Meg was once woken up after she had gone to bed so that she could have her first taste of cucumber which her uncle had brought round.

Like most other children of her age, she always remembered seeing bananas for the first time. One afternoon, when she returned home from school, her mother was waiting for her. She excitedly pushed a shopping basket with a ration book and some money into Meg's hands and told her to run to the local shop. A neighbour had told her that some crates of bananas had just been delivered.

The sight of the wooden boxes stacked on the floor of the little shop together with the patient queue of women laughing with the customers already carrying out their small bunches of bananas was later to become a defining moment in Meg's memories of the ending of the war. When she next went to visit her grandparents, she told them about having eaten her first banana and remarked that, although a banana tasted very nice, it wasn't as good as a bar of chocolate. She couldn't quite understand why all the grown-ups were so excited. Grandpa laughed and told her that for nearly six years merchant ships had battled their way across the Atlantic under terrible conditions in order to bring back supplies of much needed goods to Britain. He said that now they were able to bring back something that no one really needed at all. It signified that from now on things were going to get better. It was the unimportance of the banana that had made it so important.

As always Meg believed what Grandpa told her. She just wished she could always understand what he meant.

Things may have been getting better for the family, but they were still a long way from normal. For Meg this was not a problem. She, after all, couldn't remember any other existence. At least they now had the basics of life again: running water, gas and electricity and the children were able to play outside in the early evenings without too much worry. They were far luckier than Londoners, who were having to live with the fear of doodlebugs being aimed at the capital city from the other side of the channel. Meg learned that some London evacuees had already spent five years away from home. At least she no longer needed to worry about her own situation. There had been times, since Meg had been evacuated, when she feared she might have to go away again. It was always when she came home from school and saw her mother looking sad. The first time it happened was when she unexpectedly caught her mother sitting in the kitchen with her face buried in her hands listening to the wireless. An airliner had been shot down by the Germans. One of the passengers who had been killed was Leslie Howard, who had played Ashley in *Gone With the Wind*. He was her mother's favourite film star of all time and, probably because of his sad death, remained as such for the rest of her life.

Another time was exactly a year later when the D-day landings took place, followed in a few days by the first flying bomb attack on Britain. Her mother said the war had gone on for such a long while that it seemed as if she would never live to see the end of it.

Tuesday 8th May 1945

Meg was startled by the door at the back of the classroom being flung open. In rushed one of the older teachers who, much to Meg's amazement, had tears trickling down her face.

'The war is over,' she shouted. 'The war in Europe is over.'

Even at such an historic moment, Meg couldn't help thinking that she, herself, would have been reprimanded for such unruly behaviour.

But then this was obviously not a day for normal behaviour. Her own teacher, when she heard the news, burst into tears as did the little girl sitting across the gangway. Soon many of the other pupils were also crying. It was the first time Meg realised that people cried when they were happy as well as when they were sad. On reflection, she thought it was much better to cry with happiness.

As she left school on that memorable day, Meg skipped across the playground. She had been a very small girl when the war had begun. Now she thought of herself as almost grown-up, and in just a few short years she would be going to the big girls' school.

Today the world had changed for the better.
Tomorrow would be the start of the rest of her life.

8th June, 1946

To-day, as we celebrate victory, I send this personal message to you and all other boys and girls at school. For you have shared in the hardships and dangers of a total war and you have shared no less in the triumph of the Allied Nations.

I know you will always feel proud to belong to a country which was capable of such supreme effort; proud, too, of parents and elder brothers and sisters who by their courage, endurance and enterprise brought victory. May these qualities be yours as you grow up and join in the common effort to establish among the nations of the world unity and peace.

George R.I.

And There Was a Great Calm

Thomas Hardy
(Armistice Day)

Calm fell. From Heaven distilled a clemency;
There was peace on earth, and silence in the sky;
Some could, some could not, shake off misery:
The Sinister Spirit sneered; 'It had to be.'
And again the Spirit of Pity whispered, 'Why?'